T0108042

Jen Craig's short stories have appeared in various Australian literary magazines including *HEAT*, *Redoubt*, *Hermes* and *Southerly*. Her first novel, *Since the Accident*, was published by Ginninderra Press in 2009. She has collaborated on concert and theatre works, including the 2005 chamber opera, *A Dictionary of Maladies*, with Swiss composer Michael Schneider. Jen regularly blogs micro fiction at absurdenticements.blogspot.com and about writing and reading at beinginlieu.blogspot.com. She holds a Master of Arts in Writing from the University of Technology, Sydney, and is currently researching the relationship between writing, anorexia and the Gothic at the Writing and Society Research Centre, University of Western Sydney.

Bettina Kaiser is a visual artist as well as a graphic and web designer. She has undertaken artistic residencies in Antartica, at Arthur and Yvonne Boyd's Bundanon and in Outback Australia. She won the *2007 Hazelhurst Art on Paper Prize* and has exhibited throughout Australia as well as overseas.

PRAISE FOR JEN CRAIG

'… the reader is made aware at once that Craig is a writer of great skill.'
KERRYN GOLDSWORTHY

'Jen Craig's voice is a rare one in the field of emerging Australian literary talent. Both her novels, *Since the Accident* and *Panthers and the Museum of Fire*, exhibit a distinctive style which features careful precision of the narrative voice, coupled with an intriguing digressive approach. This draws the reader in to stories that seem endlessly reflective, yet the novels quickly display a logic and continuity that is sustained until the very last sentence.'
DEBRA ADELAIDE

'*Since the Accident* is a valuable addition to the Australian novel. It effectively realises a formal alternative to the realist tradition that dominates contemporary Australian writing, yet does so in an accessible way that deserves to find a wide readership. This ability to explore innovative novelistic form that cuts to the core of the human condition without lapsing into gratuitous experimentation is very rare, and to be highly commended.'
ANTHONY MACRIS

'*Panthers and the Museum of Fire* defies every piece of well-meant advice handed out to novelists. The language is strange and obsessive, its central character is written with no regard as to whether the reader will like or care about her, the plot is obscure and frustrating, the setting is never picturesque. And yet it succeeds brilliantly.'
ALI JANE SMITH

Panthers and the Museum of Fire

Jen Craig

Photography by Bettina Kaiser

ZEROGRAM
PRESS

Los Angeles, 2020

ZEROGRAM PRESS
An imprint of GREEN INTEGER
København / Los Angeles
2118 Wilshire Blvd. Suite #448
Santa Monica CA 90403
www.zerogrampress.com
www.greeninteger.com

Distributed by Consortium Book Sales & Distribution / Ingram Books
(800) 283-3572 / www.cbsd.com

First Zerogram Press Edition, 2020
Copyright © 2020 by Jen Craig
Cover design and photography © 2020 by Bettina Kaiser
Edited by Linda Godfrey and Annie Parkinson
Layout by Bronwyn Mehan with much-appreciated assistance by Jennifer Leung
Originally published in 2015 by Spineless Wonders
All rights reserved

LIBRARY OF CONGRESS CATALOGING-IN-PUBLICATION DATA

Names: Craig, Jen, author. | Kaiser, Bettina, illustrator.
Title: Panthers & the museum of fire / Jen Craig ; illustrated by Bettina Kaiser.
Other titles: Panthers and the museum of fire
Description: First Zerogram Press edition. | Los Angeles : Zerogram Press, 2020.
Identifiers: LCCN 2020005484 | ISBN 9781557134486 (paperback)
Classification: LCC PR9619.4.C723 P36 2020 | DDC 823/.92--dc23
LC record available at https://lccn.loc.gov/2020005484

Printed in the United States of America

For my family

PANTHERS AND THE MUSEUM OF FIRE

JEN CRAIG

For a long time I have dreamed of such a breakthrough, I thought as I set off from my flat in Glebe on that Monday morning – walking to a café in Crown Street for no other reason than to meet the sister, Pamela, so that I could give her back the manuscript *Panthers and the Museum of Fire* supposedly unread, as she had insisted on the phone only two days after she'd given it to me. I have spent years and years of my life doing little more than work towards this very breakthrough. I have sacrificed love, holidays, sanity, my health, I told myself on my way up the street from the place where the building I lived in had mired itself in the roots of Moreton Bay figs and playground urine and the foetid remnants of plastic bags – doing nothing but work and work, or at least all the time just seeming to work and work, to get close to this breakthrough that might, indeed, have always escaped me because *this* is how I find it, and in spite of myself.

It's strange, still, that I should date this breakthrough that I can now call a breakthrough from this Saturday morning only, I was thinking as I left my street behind, glad to have the hour and a half ahead of me even though I knew I wouldn't need the whole of that time to walk there. I'd stayed up all the previous night reading the manuscript – the very manuscript I had promised Pamela on the phone I wouldn't read once she had asked me not to read it, and in fact had never had any intention of reading – a detail she should have known if she'd had an ounce of sensitivity but obviously hadn't wanted to know. I finished it at half past two in the morning and then started it again. I was in a daze, nothing short of euphoria during those long, sweet hours from late on Friday to the Saturday morning, when it all became clear. At first I had been relieved to find that the manuscript was nothing – even now it seems to be nothing – and yet as I read it my mind was bated; the idea of a mind being bated in the way that breath can be bated entranced me as I walked along the narrowing part of Victoria Road where the cars, parked tight by the kerb, even crammed to the corners, made me think that everyone had been affected as I'd been affected and that no one had slept.

Although Sarah had called her manuscript *Panthers and the Museum of Fire* – or at least had written this title on the front of the manuscript, writing it in her handwriting, if in fact it was her handwriting and not someone else's – it has been so long since I can recall ever seeing her handwriting – the manuscript seemed to have nothing to do with this title: all the suggestive allure that I might have expected from a title like that. I recognised the wording at once when Pamela gave me the manuscript at Sarah's wake, passing it on to me despite my best attempts not to take it. Anyone would have recognised the wording, anyone who has ever driven along the east–west motorway of Sydney. It was the wording of a sign, of course. The title was a sign – an ordinary sign – a large white-on-brown sign that sits on the side of a road, of the sort that denotes trails or destinations of supposed tourist or heritage interest, in this case for the drivers of cars or trucks that might want to turn off the motorway to go to the rugby league club Panthers, named, as I've learned by Googling, not after the mysterious animal that is said to be wandering the Blue Mountains, confounding all attempts to capture it or even to prove it exists, but because a woman called Deidre won a competition to name the club in 1964: the name Panthers being only one of her many suggestions, her many animal-name suggestions. The sign on the motorway directs you to Panthers, where you can play the pokies, eat, buy caps or T-shirts or banded scarves in the Panthers' colours and so be able to imagine that you are running out on the field in front of a crowd, an obvious faithful of the Panthers rugby league team, or a Panther yourself, a colossus in shorts that embodies the hopes and dreams of thousands – driving to the massive, gleaming building that is the club today, or to the Museum of Fire, where you can buy caps or T-shirts (again) and so imagine you are speeding through lights and overtaking the police in search of a fire that is flaming in secret, fearsome lines of fire that everyone wants put out and yet everyone, too, would prefer to watch as they burn and burn forever – this sign that for years I have known to be nothing more than a sign on a road, and even followed once, in a moment of willed spontaneity and determined flair – a moment that might have changed my life.

The fact that this sign was the title of the manuscript I had been given had affected me from the start in the way that this sign on the road has always affected me. Take the route number fourteen, the sign tells us, and you will get to these places, these ordinary yet wide, bright places that I know to be there, or instead, as I might once have wanted, you will drive out of this existence into a tunnel of darkness, where every possibility ripens in the night. I might make light of the white-on-brown sign that I've seen for myself on any number of occasions; I might make light of this sign, in thoughts such as these – I might even make light of the contrast between the suggestive, alluring wording of the sign that I have always remarked on when I've driven past it, and the ordinary, merchandised places that it refers to – entertaining my good friend Raf, as I am always trying to entertain him, with thoughts such as these, saving them up for the times I see him – and yet I know that to say this is all I think of this sign (and the manuscript) would not be the truth.

Perhaps, quite apart from anything else, it could have been that the reference to this sign and the wording of the sign – the entire coincidence of this sign and the manuscript and the death of the author of it – the one-time friend from my years at high school – had moved my mind into a state of euphoria as I read the manuscript once and then twice within hours of the call from

the sister, Pamela, in which case, she would have been interested
to know this, I told myself as I walked towards her and the café
where she'd arranged for us to meet that Monday. At the wake,
she would have loved to hear such a thing – at the time when she
still wanted me to read the manuscript, when she had imposed on
me this reading of the manuscript, when she wanted, as she no
longer evidently does, to believe that *something special could come
from her sister* – but even then I knew that I had to be careful what
I said to her. Over the years, I have learned to be careful and this
is an instinctive reaction – almost a physiological reaction. There
is a certain sort of person that it might be said I have a definite
allergy to, as I explained to Raf when he came over for dinner
last night. Already once in my life I have allowed myself to be
far too free with the expression of my thoughts near Pamela and
people like Pamela, I mused as I pulled a sharp-edged, waxy leaf
from one of the hedges I was walking past – one of those tasteful,
box-shaped hedges that Glebe is full of – a leaf whose webbed
underside reminded me of the peculiar setting of the *house party*
that I had described to Raf the day before, and so the physiological
and psychological sensations of my one-time *religious conversion.*

But I have to realise that the euphoria I remember after reading
the manuscript – the whole time sitting in the chair with the arms
that I keep near the window for the purpose of reading – that this
euphoria was experienced more as a relief than excitement or in
any way a breakthrough in the sense that I am thinking of it now.
It was more a large, relieved sigh, a sound travelling out of me, as if
the air that had stayed in my mind through those first and second
readings had been released in one go, and as such the euphoria
itself was not so much a dazed excitement, as I am reinventing it
now, but a release of air, of anxiety, of the preparedness that I had
brought to the manuscript that supposedly I had to read at one
time – my preparedness for something undefined but threatening,
very evidently threatening to my self. It was extraordinary that
I should have felt so relieved, I was thinking as I crossed to the
sunnier side of Allen Street only seconds before a van swung in

silence around the corner behind me, nearly pushing me into the stationary cars – a large white van whose blinking flicker continued too fast and for far too long, stunned for the moment, to watch this van that kept on moving in its massive, rattling, unnerving absence of sound. Yes, I began to think again, forcing myself to return to my earlier reflections, so as not to be diverted from what I was trying now to understand as I walked towards Pamela and the café in Crown Street – given how I had been feeling about the manuscript and the circumstances surrounding the passing on to me of the manuscript at the wake – and about the one-time, now deceased friend who had written it, to whom I had hardly spoken in years, as I explained to Raf last night, and whom I could still not tally with the coffin – the contents of the coffin – that disappeared while we were all being distracted by a song that went, as I told him: *Nothing compares to you* (he might even remember this song, it was years and years old but very popular at the time) – it was strange that it should have been relief that I experienced after reading the manuscript, considering that it was only my old friend Sarah who had written it – a relief that was euphoria, a euphoric relief.

You have to imagine a book, I should have told my friend – a book but not a book – the fact that it was a manuscript made a difference. The whole time that you were reading this manuscript that was not yet a book, you would have found the experience of reading just an experience of waiting; the whole time that you were reading, you were also waiting. As soon as you started the manuscript, you would find yourself waiting for it to start, to *really start*. You kept flicking pages and reading and flicking – not skipping any pages, but flicking them all the same – and the whole time you reading you were waiting for the story in the manuscript to *start for real*. This feeling, you have to realise, kept up the whole time. There was a never a moment when you thought you had started on the section of the manuscript where the real part began. At first you would have been flicking the pages and thinking, well she could have cut these paragraphs and all of these pages here, cut all of it so far, and yet this feeling of needing to cut most of what you were reading persisted until the end. In fact, the whole of the reading seemed to be just the prelude to a reading; it pulled you along from one sentence to the next, one paragraph to the next, and you held on for some reason, never doubting for an instant that the real part of the story would be about to begin; and even when you knew, later on, when it was evidently too late, *that there was no real part* – when you watched yourself holding on to your role in the reading like an idiotic fool, holding on for the real part to begin when all the time there was never a real part, all the time there was nothing but the reading of the manuscript one word after another, the words being everything, the storyline nothing – you continued to read, I should have told Raf last night, although I was still jet-lagged, if I could call it that, from the experience of reading and writing. It was the most idiotic thing, but you continued to read.

I rang Raf when, having put down the manuscript for the third or fourth time yesterday and written for hours like the day before – that is to say, not quite straight after my breakthrough, which had occurred on Saturday – writing for hours again, as I had done through the night, and not being sure any more of what I was doing, or why I was doing it, and needing to do something then – anything at all – to walk out from my flat, from the manuscript and my writing – to shop, I was remembering now – I knew I needed an excuse to shop so I might escape for a moment from all that reading and writing. I rang my friend Raf because I had to do something, my restlessness having become impossible now (impossible to sleep, impossible to think), to invite him over at the last minute, telling myself as I pressed in the numbers (my fingers not so much numb but failing to feel), that this is what we always do; our ringing of each other at the last minute has become a habit over the years, even an assertion of our difference from everybody else – our particular source of pride – that we never plan our rendezvous more than twenty-four hours in advance (when in fact, we have often given days, even weeks of notice, I was realising as I emerged from the backstreets onto Glebe Point Road and crossed to the pharmacy, to its tall panes of glass that held me along with the stripes on the road for a moment and then, as the shade cut the sun, seemed to swallow me whole). Other people need schedules and plan their social life weeks and weeks in advance, I had told myself as I listened to the ringing of his phone in my phone as I waited in my flat, but we are still spontaneous, as we have said to each other on many occasions. So much of life is drained of spontaneity. The older people get, the tighter they get, their skin becomes loose but their minds just tighten like drums. We have always refused to tighten – we continue to stay loose and spontaneous. Others can start getting out their phones, their laptops, and send themselves messages about dinners and arrangements that hem them all around, but we have always stopped at such idiocy. All these years we have preferred to grab occasions on the fly – whole evenings, whole days, without thinking of the cost. It's what keeps us young and flexible in our minds. Everyone thinks that both of us are younger than we are and this is the reason. We have always refused to grow rigid and tight. Other people succumb but we resist. If we tried blocking in our arrangements in advance we would never get to see each other, I had been thinking while I waited on the phone, still high, as I might have called it, from all that reading and writing and, more importantly, from the enormity of my breakthrough, and wanting now to talk to Raf or to anyone who would listen. I wanted to go out and get walking, and so going out to shop for a dinner with Raf was the perfect way to do it. You should come as early as you feel like, I had said to him on the phone, when he had at last picked up with his usual terse, always ironic and tentative hello – five-thirty, six: whatever. It's your call. I'm up to my neck in stuff, I said, so I won't be so prepared, but you are used to my mess after all. I will try to get back from the shops as early as I can. I've laid down a sparkling, and a couple of Coopers. It's been ages since we last caught up – so much has happened, and all of it strange.

It was only a year or two ago that I had first mentioned Sarah to him – that old friend from school that I might have forgotten had I not run into her on the street one day, a street completely out of my usual orbit, as I'd said to Raf that time we were at a Potts Point pub, where we'd been *testing the kitchen* (Raf being an occasional reviewer of places like these even now that I'm writing this five or six years on, when the new work he's doing in St Leonards leaves him no time, as he puts it when I call him, to scratch his arse). I had been walking along a street in Rockdale because I'd had to go to Rockdale to get my printer fixed, and I had been musing about how different Rockdale was from anywhere else I usually went in Sydney and I'd been wondering who on earth lived in Rockdale or plied their business in Rockdale where, past the main intersection, at a vista of descending apartments each with a view, I was sure, of a wide grey ocean – I could sense it in the changing density of the air – I knew I had arrived at a beachside suburb which, far from exciting me, depressed me to the core. The shop where I was taking my printer to get fixed was on the main street of Rockdale and I hadn't been able to park right in front of it, I told Raf across the table at the pub – the pub that he had been wanting to check out after the renovations that had cost a full million, which he could hardly believe since it looked complete crap. I told him that I'd parked a good block or more beyond it, on the other side of the street, and it was just after I'd crossed the street and was heading towards the shop with my printer in my arms that I saw Sarah, this old friend from high school, coming towards me on the same side. I remember how at first I hadn't recognised her – or, more specifically, that I was so taken aback by seeing what I only realised at the very last minute to be her that I was ready to keep walking right past her, with my printer taking all of my attention (in fact the cord had kept slipping out of my hands and the prop for the paper had already half fallen out). I might have kept walking, trying to ignore her, as I could have been so busy, given the circumstances with the cord and the prop not to mention my thoughts, that I might not have seen her in the first place – but this, I had realised in an instant, would have made me regretful afterwards, as it has always made me regretful when, not out of cowardice so much as an insuperable laziness, I let myself slide into a duplicity that I would not recognise as such – my mind being ever and always ready to believe what I would never believe if it came from anyone else – so much kinder, more indulgent, as I am, I was thinking at the time, of my self. Some of this I might have said to Raf – or perhaps I hadn't – but I had explained how across my preoccupation with the cord and the prop – or my seeming preoccupation with the cord and the prop – Sarah had cut through to me with the kind of greeting that I hadn't heard in years. Sarah called me Jenny, of course, which nobody but my parents call me these days – my parents preferring to ignore the fact that they had called their daughter after, though in advance of, a multinational dieting company, I had said to Raf who immediately laughed as I was hoping he would – and so Sarah called me Jenny and I had to stop walking and say hello.

Sarah has always been someone, I said to Raf that time, I was remembering now as I was walking towards Pamela in the café in Surry Hills – hurrying to make it to the lights at St Johns Road because I could see that, for the traffic heading in my direction, they had just turned orange and so were threatening to stop me, and I didn't want to stop – that in fact I had been so much sucked into my thoughts that I might instead, all this time, have been hurrying up the steeper part of the highway going north at Rockdale than south past the trays of tomatoes and lemons and broccolini in Glebe I was careful to avoid even as I was now running towards the changing lights at St Johns Road. Sarah, you have to understand, I had said to Raf a couple of years ago in that pub, I now remembered as I ran in front of a car that was turning down the hill before the lights went red – Sarah has always been someone devoid of irony. The day I was sent to the office to meet the new girl in Year Eight to bring her back to roll call, I might have interpreted this girl's manner – her way of speaking with abrupt conviction through a face that didn't move – such a heavy, dry manner, as of someone who is always making jokes, always sending herself up, and yet never makes jokes (at least, none that I can remember) – I might have interpreted this manner as a great, unreserved, and very general criticism of everything she had ever seen in the world (which in a way it was, very likely). I might have taken it personally, at the time – as a criticism of me, of the school – I had heard, from the teacher, that she had had to leave *an exclusive private school* – but for some reason I had warmed to this manner, or if not warmed to it, found myself loosening as I accompanied her from the administrative block to our roll call classroom. She said nothing to me at the office, not even smiling when we were introduced, and as we made our way along the covered walkways to roll call, she hardly said more than three or four words. At one point I stopped in the courtyard – I had stopped to show her the tower with the bell that was also an incinerator and the canteen beyond it – telling her about the queues and when to avoid the queues, and the time I'd found a cockroach in my icy pole and how the lockers in the corner always smelled of urine, because someone kept pissing there, though nobody yet had been caught in the act – the kind of information, I realised then I had an anxious, uncontrolled pleasure in relating, the grossness of the anecdotes disturbing me less than the certainty I was indulging a weakness in my self, and her response, which had sounded abrupt – I don't remember the wording, only that her response had been abrupt, even rude, like a shove, but also irrelevant, completely *something else* – this response, far from exposing me to my self, had somehow eased me – what a relief, I had thought, at least I don't need to keep turning these same anecdotes over. No necessity to talk – or more, no necessity to agonise over the content of what I say. I might have been offended, but instead I was relieved. It was uncomplicated hanging around with Sarah in those days, I might have said to Raf, or so it occurred to me as I walked down Glebe Point Road, past the breach in the shopfronts that I've always thought of as the *un*-Glebe section, and becoming uncertain now about what exactly I had said or hadn't said that time to Raf in the Potts Point pub. She didn't make friends very easily I could see, and, in fact, I didn't like her much – there was very little to like – but it was easy to hang around with her all the same, to shelter behind the abrupt shove of her voice, her unlikeable directness and the huge, uncompromising silence that she seemed to prefer to speaking and that suited me well I have to say, as I probably told my friend Raf. But I know, I went on to tell him, it's hard being an adolescent. I would never want to be an adolescent again – at least not the adolescent that I was: too timid to disrupt the ritual exchange of expected opinions, too fearful of losing the all that was already eluding me, too naïve to doubt that the scent of certain leaves in autumn or blossoms in winter and the whole bush gully experience could be anything other than the essence of the life my parents had bought in that supposedly safe and family-oriented area in the 1960s and that I was anxious never to lose. It was a relief to hang around with Sarah in those days. When I was with my other friends I would bitch about Sarah – saying things like she is so depressing, doesn't she get you down? She's a brain but it's hard to take, she just hangs around – I can't do anything about her hanging around. But, in fact, I liked to hang around with Sarah, I'm sure I said to Raf back then, the whole time aware as I was saying it of the occasions when Raf had told similar stories of doing time, as we both put it, *in outer suburbia*. It was a relief hanging around with Sarah, a blessed relief. Hanging around with Sarah was my only relief. And yet even as I said this to Raf, I realised now that I was walking along the northern side of Glebe Point Road, past the shop whose windows of seventies chunky cups and delicate tints of depression glassware always made me feel unaccountably cheered – even though I had expressed all this to Raf in the pub that was way overpriced for what we got, as he had said – the piddling salads, the basil-less pesto – I had known that the relief I had felt back then was rather a guilty relief. It was true that it was a relief. I was not wrong in describing it as a relief, I told myself as I walked past the garden-fronted café whose windows were still boarded up with sheets of scabrous ply, and yet I knew all the time that this relief was tarnished, as I should have put it, by my enjoyment of everything I used to do with Sarah away from school: all the trips to the cinema, her parents paying, rides on the horses she kept at a family friend's place in Dural, weeks at their beach house, her cast-off records, her Agatha Christie novels, interesting, complicated games, clothing which I admired more than she ever did – the: are you sure? I used to say with my devious politeness every time; are you sure you don't want it? I did everything a poor kid could do in the company of a rich kid, I could have said, although even this would not be the absolute truth. I will never be able to get to the bottom of the truth about my friendship with Sarah, there being neither glamour, nor interest, nor sex, nor anything at the base of it save my self and only my self; everything that suited me when it suited me because: didn't I avoid her the moment that it didn't suit me, I asked myself as I passed the tables of books outside Sappho's and Gleebooks and could already see the people who were sitting at what looked to be a continuous run of cafés ahead on the foot-path under the awnings – some of the people with their dogs tied to the chair legs, others standing near them as if they had only just come across from somewhere else to talk, as I might have done myself if I wanted to, if I had the nerve, if I knew even one of the people or wanted to pretend I did – this crowding that I loved, this walking among strangers who will, forever, stay strangers, but also a crowding that, now that I had crossed the side street and was walking among it – rather than only *thinking* of walking among it – I wanted to shrink from, because the moment I heard the words the people at the tables were using, I knew that each of their words might have been mine and that there was something about the shaded faces in fresh-looking clothes that, coupled with those tedious verbal expressions that I often used myself, those same few phrases – those *really greats*, those *I've been thinkings* and *wonderings* – all those phrases that I would expunge if I could – that there was something about them that mimicked how I have always found myself feeling. It was not so much a friendship as an exploitation, I would have said a year or more ago to Raf had I realised it then.

But it would have been difficult to explain all of this to my friend Raf even if I had wanted to, I realised as I continued to walk towards the corner of Glebe Point Road and Parramatta Road. Analysing thoughts – particularly thoughts like these – takes time and patience, and even then, the analysis itself is only ever likely to be provisional. Each time I have tried to analyse my thoughts, I have begun in one direction, seeing connections, tracing the lines that lead from one thought to another; all would be clear in that direction. I would always be amazed. How is it that I have never seen it in this way before, I would ask myself; how is it that it has taken all these years to discover this simply patterned shape that is the reality of my life? Too many times, I have come to these sorts of conclusions, only to set the conclusions aside somewhere, like the way jottings on a scrap of paper are set on a shelf, next to the phone or under a jumble of papers in the kitchen, only to be found much later and promptly thrown out, the jottings themselves now indecipherable or embarrassingly naïve, all thoughts of this kind soon becoming indecipherable or naïve. All I had done that evening with Raf was to describe the abrupt, strange nature of my old friend's voice – the extraordinary way that this voice could cut through and yet, in itself, be blunt. I had imitated this voice of my old friend Sarah, the way she had called me Jenny, although making it shriller and more stupid sounding than it had been: more canting and shrill, a kind of false falsetto – a woman imitating a man who is imitating a woman. I had got a laugh from my good friend Raf when I imitated Sarah calling out to me despite my best efforts to ignore her in Rockdale, with a cord that I would have preferred to be writhing in my hands – in the way that a child who squirms and cries in a public place gives the mother a chance to show that she takes her job as a parent more seriously than others might expect of her; I am someone who has to carry a printer, who has to fit the repair of a printer into her already busy day. I am hurrying with my printer. I have to get my printer to the repairers because I'm sick of all the waste in this society that we live in, the infinite accumulation of waste that I'm always going on about – and they don't even provide a parking space for customers out the front – but Sarah had seen through me as it were, I was realising now as I got closer to the corner of Glebe Point Road and Parramatta Road, where the noise, building slowly into a long continuum of scraping and squealing and hissing as I walked, was as soothing as I was expecting it to be, but also not as loud. She had stopped me with my name – her pronunciation of it perfectly raw and flat, innocent of innuendo – and I had responded with an intensity: a barrage of verbal invention that was an effort of feigned and so exaggerated, heart-felt polite expression, about how great it was to see her, how busy I had been, how ridiculous this business with the printer and the repairers and the way the whole system of computer technology had us running continually from one place to another, always an update that crashed the software, that made it impossible to keep up with all the other never-ending things that we had to do every minute of the day – about how disastrous was our dependence on these fragile, plastic parts, since none of us would last more than a week without any of this technology we were always complaining about, because even the simplest thing, even a loaf of bread…

And from this I distilled the account for Raf in the pub of my running into Sarah in Rockdale – that old friend I might once have mentioned to you: *she was the one that lived in that huge glitzy house higher in the gully from where I lived and who I used to hang around with at high school even though we didn't have a thing in common, not a single interest: it was just a relief to hang around with her in contrast to what else was happening at that time in my life* (about which I have never given details of any sort to Raf – nor even begun to understand for myself). I imitated the way she had called out Jenny: the way she waited, watching me, as I had said to Raf across the small pale wooden table in that pub in Potts Point, *already oppressing me with that intense and depressing way she has about her* so there was nothing I could do. I had to promise that we would catch up soon. I wrote her number down. I even told her not to take offence if I didn't phone her in the next two or three weeks, there being so much that had cropped up that I was run off my feet, but if she could give me her number I would call her a little while after that, when everything had settled down and we could meet for a chat. But, of course, as I had said to Raf that first time I'd talked about Sarah, I still can't imagine ringing her – I couldn't imagine it then when I was speaking, nor later in the car. We always put off making calls like these and it is not because I never intended ringing her – it was never like that – at the time I was genuine in my desire to ring her, even against my own resistance, and had in fact been foolhardy enough, given the circumstances, to ask her to wait two or three weeks. And yet that was at least being honest, more honest than I could have been. I could just have said, I suppose, that I was going to ring her – everybody does that – but I was genuinely busy for those two or three weeks. I knew I was busy, and so to tell her I was busy then was only to be straight with her. But by saying this I have made it all the more necessary that I ring her, I had said to Raf when I wanted his advice back then, or at least his commiseration. Having given her this schedule – a specific number of weeks – I know I have to stick to what I said. If I hadn't said that I was too busy in the next few weeks, she could have assumed that my offer of ringing her was only the equivalent of every other offer to ring her, every other empty offer, and when I don't end up ringing her, I might be excused because I would just have merged with all the others who have ever made offers to ring her – all the other offers to ring that are casually given and casually received, and are always understood from the outset to be nothing more than nothing. I have really put myself into it, I'd said, by being so specific about the number of weeks. I should never have mentioned that I would be busy for that period of time, but now that I have mentioned it I really should ring her – it's vital that I ring her – it's what I have to do. It has become a weight on my mind, I had admitted to Raf by way of entertainment – in the way that we are always entertaining each other with stories of this kind. But of course I was told in that pub what I knew all along Raf would say, I was remembering now that I had turned the corner of Glebe Point Road full into the noise and the wind and was walking into the wide, flapping sheets of sun along Parramatta Road: my friend Raf telling me that surely she wouldn't be expecting me to ring, that nobody would, despite that caveat of the number of weeks, since just saying that you were going to ring someone in the future at all was an obvious flick and she would have to be an idiot if she thought any differently; Raf saying that this was the way everyone did it, this saying you were going to ring – she wasn't born yesterday – because hadn't I just told him I didn't want to see her? – wasn't she boring and dull, too boring to bother with? – I should just get over that feeling, that sense of being obliged, as this kind of encounter is the stuff of everyday life. Every day, I remember him saying, people promise to ring someone in such a way that everyone concerned knows the promise to be a lie. Nobody in their right mind ever takes a promise like that at face value, and so it's more fool me to believe I am beholden. Even your friend, he told me as we stood up to take leave of the pub: even your friend wouldn't have taken the promise at face value – the way he said 'your friend' giving the whole story of my encounter with Sarah a particularly unpleasant savour, I was realising on Parramatta Road as I hurried towards the building site that was once a church near the corner of Mountain Street – whose legendary fire, it was said, had been started by someone who had finally had enough of the church, of the repeated attempts by the church on his soul – this use of the words 'your friend' very likely making me reluctant to think too much about what I should or shouldn't do in the weeks that followed seeing Sarah in Rockdale and putting a stop to any further thoughts about it and so encouraging me, I realised as I hurried past the tiny newsagency with its already soiled and battered posters in their cages on the wall, to avoid making a decision of any sort whatsoever until it was too late of course, since Sarah is dead.

As I pushed by the people at the bus stop this side of the remnant of that burnt-out church, I remembered how obsessed I had been, only the day before, about what I should say about Sarah. Everything that I said about Sarah and the promised phone call will come back to Raf when I tell him about her death and funeral, I had thought as I prepared for his coming over to my place last night. It's been a year or two, possibly more, since I saw her in Rockdale, but as soon as I mention this one-time friend, and describe her voice (again imitating the way she had called me Jenny, just to jog his memory), he will be sure to remember what I had said about her the last time. I'm in shock about this death – and more: there is guilt in my shock, a great smothering of guilt – and yet I can't even try to appear to be shocked and upset by the death of my one-time friend when I see Raf, I was thinking yesterday afternoon when I got back from the shops – this new term 'one-time friend' making it easier for me to think of her and the situation with any kind of equanimity. Raf is sure to point out to me my hypocrisy if I appear to be shocked, no matter how genuinely affected I might be when I tell him about the death and funeral of this friend of mine who was the exact same age as me and had gone to the same high school and smelled the same raging but always distant bushfires through our teenage summers, which were precisely the same summers, no less humid or hot or more interesting than the other person's summers, except for the detail of the one of us having had so much more access, as it's put, to so many more advantages; one being so much better off in a material way than the other; and yet also there is pleasure in the anticipation of telling Raf about this death and funeral, I had realised yesterday when I returned from the shops with my neatly wrapped kilo of prawns to prepare for his coming. I've so much to say. The Germans have a word to describe this pleasure but I can't think of what it is; the Germans have a word but I have a sense that their word is more malicious and gleeful than the pleasure I am imagining. There is a pleasure in the telling of a story like this, and particularly a sad or depressing story that has details of irony or surprise. That German word I am trying to remember could not possibly encompass the welling and, at base, wilful determination to talk of such a pleasure – a description of which difference I would love to indulge in even though I have no knowledge at all about this word, and so a reference to it, in the company of Raf at least, even in an ironic and laughing, self-deprecating way, would only be pretentious. As tempting as it is to try to be clever when I see him, I shouldn't even mention this German word reference, I remember telling myself as I began to peel the onions to accompany the prawns. The moment I overstep the elaboration of what I tell I always regret it – Raf never fails to point it out when what I say is inaccurate or exaggerated. The number of times that this has happened should be enough to make me beware of such a temptation. Raf himself never fails to point out anyone's stupidities and so the fact that I am always surprised when it happens to me is a stupidity in itself. The number of times I have left his flat, knowing that I have blundered, knowing that I have said the most stupid inanities, obvious inanities – he must often discuss me with his own friends afterwards, I had only then realised as I used my fingernail to remove the resistant parts of the onion skin – one of the many friends I have never met but have been told, very likely, everything about. I have probably known, unconsciously, for years that he does this, and yet I always ring my old friend Raf and want to see him and tell him things.

In the end, as it happened, it was easy to talk to Raf about Sarah's death. I was now walking further down the slope along Parramatta Road – a road that soon somewhere, I knew, changed its name to Broadway. I had crossed with the lights at Mountain Street and was worrying just a little as I used always to worry about the intersection to come – the one with no lights or pedestrian crossing at the south end of Wattle Street where, as I would say to Raf and some of the people I knew at work when I still lived in Glebe, *you take your life in your hands*. Words like 'death' and 'funeral' are in fact very easy to say, I told myself as I looked in at the shop that had only a few sets of unusually small women's shoes in the window. This is easier than I expected, I even remember thinking as I was talking to Raf last night not long after he arrived: here I am telling the story of Sarah's death and funeral and I am not being affected in any way at all – the performance of these two words is itself invigorating. Someone has died and someone has been cremated; it is the end of life, of all existence for someone I used to know quite well, and yet here I am using the words 'death' and 'funeral' as if they mean nothing but a reference to my connection with a well-known drama that is being enacted elsewhere (in the cinema, for example). Someone has died and this someone I have betrayed by making light of her existence in my talk to my friend. And yet, the fact of this death and this betrayal means nothing, even less than nothing, I'd thought as I described for Raf last night first hearing about the death on the phone from the sister, Pamela, and then going to the funeral: the abrupt, unexpected news of the death and the ordinary, too ordinary, event of the funeral.

Pamela guessed that I probably hadn't been in touch with Sarah for a while, I had told Raf when he came over to my place on the Sunday. As I walked past a series of shops that sold telephone plans, I recalled yet again what Pamela had said during the wake, and how much I had enjoyed relating to Raf this exchange we had had. Pamela had said I would hardly have recognised her sister these last few years before she died, it was so, so sad. Sarah had changed so much. She had become, did I know, *quite a lot larger*. She had never taken good care of herself, and this problem had only grown worse. Pamela had been worried about Sarah. She had worried constantly and for a number of reasons, but family can only *do so much* – no matter what she suggested, Sarah did her own thing – she could be amazingly stubborn, and so although the family were *shocked at her passing*, they weren't that surprised. They had done what they could but Sarah hadn't wanted to have a bar of any of their ideas, even when they had banded together and offered to pay for gym and swimming pool memberships, personal trainers, Weight Watchers programs, digital step counters, live-in-camps (in *regenerating rural environments*), Wii video games, even a spot on *The Biggest Loser* through a contact at work. And, of course, it was at this point that Pamela had looked at me, I told Raf as I shelled the prawns in front of him, involving him in the meal as soon as he arrived (Raf was rinsing the prawns after I'd gutted them and then patting them dry with piece after piece of paper towel) – this sister looking at me or if not quite at me, somewhere close to my head, even half a metre back, a change coming over her face as if only, at that moment, she had realised something that was vital – looking in my direction as she asked me whether I had changed my name – hinting at my name, my full although short-ened name as she had known it once, and then saying it aloud with a sly show of innocence and an obvious smirk – she was sorry, she said, she had never realised it before – and it was the kind of smirk that I recognised from long years of hearing and seeing such smirks on account of my name. Every time someone smirks in this way, I told Raf, I can tell they are congratulating themselves for *being on the ball* and I hear these congratulations, these suppressed and so palpable self-congratulations. You have only known me since university, and so only since I had been robbed of my name by that weight loss company – a loss that I have never got over, as I've said before, on any number of occasions – because laughably – and this I have also said many times over – at the time of the launch of the company I had been anorexic, *a bag of pathetic stick bones*, as a neighbour of my parents' had once called me to my mother in the garden. You first got to know me at university not long after I was anorexic – or in fact while I was still anorexic – and my name was a mockery, I reminded him yesterday, and so your getting to know me and having to accept the mockery of my name during those new, early days of the diet company, while I still walked the country as a bag of stick bones with a diet company's name – or the diet company had named itself after me, the bag of stick bones – all this had occurred at the same time. I could have changed my name, of course, as I've said before, I had gone on to say. At the time so many people advised me to change my name, yourself included – do you remember? Very likely not. But I was anorexic at that time and so I refused to listen to what they and you were saying. No anorectic can bear advice, and particularly no advice that touches on or even seems to touch on our inviolate selves. I know I have probably said much of this before, but I know that many people don't understand this, can never understand this, which is why the problem of anorexia is only getting worse and worse. Anorectics are hypersensitive to any remark that seems to relate to their bodies as selves – not so much their bodies as such, but their bodies as the visible part of the self they are doing their utmost to protect from the inquisition of everyone else. There are a lot of theories in the world about anorexia, and most of them are useless. Every doctor, every parent, every sister, every friend, every busybody neighbour has an opinion on anorexia; every psychiatrist, every counsellor, every cook, every friend of a friend. All those who haven't been anorexic themselves have no idea about anorexia because they have never led an anorexic existence, and it is the anorexic existence – the nature of this existence – the primacy of this existence – which matters more than anything else in the world to an anorectic. An anorectic needs to exist in this way because there is nothing else in their existence but existence itself; everything else in the world they have given up for this existence; the anorectic is an addict of the anorexic existence. The fact that many such existences come to grief in a premature death is neither here nor there for the anorectic. I know that in the past you have accused me of exaggerating the situation, both exaggerating the situation and the logic of the anorectic, but the anorectic is already in an exaggerated state; the anorectic is already an exaggeration. The existence that anorectics have chosen and continue to maintain for themselves at great cost to themselves is the one and only thing that they can be sure of in the world and so the fact that this existence will soon, in the course of things – and directly as a result of this existence – extinguish itself – a fact that no one ever hides from anorectics but instead uses as a weapon against them as often as they can – the supposed fact that an anorexic existence will soon, very directly, lead to a ceasing of that existence, even this anorexic existence, is hardly a matter of importance to them. The existence of anorectics is whole, entire, and they know that this wholeness and entirety will persist until the moment of death – that is, until the end of existence, their existence – which is all that they are asking for. Anorectics don't ask much of this world; all they ask is to be left to themselves in their anorexic existence, which they have chosen themselves for themselves and for nobody else. Anorectics require little more of life than that they might be free to maintain the anorexia they have chosen in their highly magnified – or if you like, exaggerated – way, but nobody ever leaves them alone in this state. You will find, instead, that no one can resist attempting to interfere with the life of an anorectic. Look around you – although now, I admit, you would have to go quite a distance to see an anorectic – you would have to go out to schools, to beaches, to gyms, to libraries in the suburbs, to solitary paths behind car parks – you couldn't just stay in our own little circle here in the city to see an anorectic – but if you were able to find one you would see, just as quickly, that this girl – and they are usually girls, although not always – this girl is always surrounded by busybodies and interferers. Many of the busybodies and inter-ferers are her own parents or the friends and colleagues of her parents, but just as many of them are her own age and purport to be her friends. The busybodies and interferers are always passing judgement on an anorectic and they are unable to keep to them-selves the judgement they make, for one reason: that they assume it is always the anorectic who is wrong and they who are right; that the perspective of the anorectic is, by definition, distorted, and that their own perspective, again by their own definition, clear and true. Although it is correct – I had reminded Raf, I thought as I hurried towards the Wattle Street intersection which I dreaded – that the anorectic is already, on her own, in an exaggerated state, this is not the same as saying that her perspective is distorted. Everything about the existence of an anorectic is exaggerated, from the wholeness of her existence to the threat to her self in a single thawed pea, and yet this is far from saying that she has a distorted perspective. When I was an anorectic, myself, my existence was perfect. Seen now, from the perspective of now, this is only an exaggeration, not at all a distortion. Looking back, I know that I exaggerated the perfection of the existence I had made for myself as an anorectic, but I also remember that my existence, during those months and years, was as perfect as it has ever been in all the years since I stopped being an anorectic; that during those years when I was anorexic, my existence was as complete and inviolable – in fact more complete and inviolable – than it has ever been since. I had to wrench my self from my anorexic existence to be free of it. In fact, I had to kill the self that was anorexic. I could have no pity. I had to decide for myself to force my self to understand my self, and it was only in this way that I could throttle the anorectic. I was surrounded, as is every anorectic, by the scourge of busybodies and interferers – and particularly since my neighbour, who was four years younger, and so *impressionable*, as my mother had told me – particularly since this neighbour had seemed to contract anorexia not long after I did, my influence becoming a baleful, malicious, conniving influence, or so I'd heard the mother accusing *my* mother one evening as she stood on the doorstep with a pair of pruning shears in one hand, some ropes of purple flowering lantana in the other – and so it was only when I was able to be free of this scourge in any way possible – as luck would have it the family next door soon moved away, but the girl never recovered, as I heard, and *died in care* only a few months later – it was only by keeping my self to the house, refusing to go out, that I had any chance whatsoever in throttling the anorectic. Had the busybodies and interferers succeeded in swaying me in any way at all I would still be an anorectic today. I might have emerged for a time and then submerged a year later – I might have emerged and submerged any number of times; I might have become that impossible long-lived anorectic, that too sweet, too vapid, too devious mind. As it was, I decided myself to kill the anorectic; none of this you would have understood from knowing me then, I had said very directly to Raf; none of this could you have possibly found out from anybody else. According to my parents, the local general practitioner *did wonders*. The fact that she was a complete and utter idiot and insufferable in her self-congratulations over the supposedly clever plan she had devised – her clever plan that I should write a daily list of what I ate and so match it up to a recommended plan, which I only ever falsified to her total gullibility (the insult, I had thought, that she could think that it would work) – only adds to my irritation with this falsifying tale, and yet I have always allowed them to think that the local general practitioner saved me from anorexia. Over the years I have listened to the tale of how the local general practitioner was a saviour. I have heard my parents recommend her to friends of others, to the children of friends of friends – and yet I have never once told them how wrong they are. It is the last thing I would ever want to tell them. Let them take the credit – with the doctor – that they saved me from anorexia, and they will never learn the truth about my anorexia. They and the doctor can take the credit for saving me from anorexia if it means that they leave my thoughts and me alone to themselves. It is my thoughts and I that are paramount in this case. I cannot bear – and I have never been able to bear, at any time in my life – any interference with my self – particularly my thoughts. It was this anxiety on behalf of my self, and hence my thoughts, which in fact convinced me that I had to kill the anorectic. When it came to a choice between my body as experience and my thoughts as experience I had to choose my thoughts. There was nothing else to be done. Until I decided to be done with the anorectic, I was always being interfered with by supposed well-wishers, friends and friends of my parents – as well as people who are only out to accuse anorectics, like those neighbours of my parents, whose daughter, as I remember, was so cowed by their meddling, so anxious to live (and die) as she wanted, that I would catch her watching me from her room in the house next door through the bare stick branches in the trees between us, sitting so still, in such complete concentration, that if I moved, I knew, she would hardly notice, even as I knew she was watching me and had always done this. Anything anybody said, at that stage, was interpreted invariably – by my self, or more specifically, my anorexic self – as an intrusion into that self, an attempt to interfere; an invitation from my friends to go out I would always know to be an attempt by them – in conspiracy with my parents – to assault my body, to stuff my anorexic self with whatever food they could find, which would dull my self, making thoughts impossible; an invitation to the movies – as an attempt to brainwash or to distract me from my self; a book, ditto; a chat, ditto; as I've said before, the busybodies and interferers that surround an anorectic cannot control themselves when it comes to intruding and interfering. Have you ever heard of someone who leaves an anorectic alone? Of course, any advice to change my name at that time I would have interpreted as an intrusion and interference – because how else were these others interpreting what was happening but through the state of my self made visible and vulnerable to them by the apparent consequences of my anorexia? The fact that my name happened to coincide, then, with a newly formed multinational dieting company could not be a fact that was left to itself, a momentary irritation, but needed to be brought to my situation, as I saw it, and interpreted through the anorexic visible self that they were always watching. It is very likely that the coincidence was more disturbing to others – to my parents and the busybodies – than it ever was to me, because the fact that others began repeatedly urging me to change my name – and this repeated urging on the part of others, however much I might have wanted to change my name as a result of my own irritation with the coincidence, meant that I became more and more adamant in refusing to do anything about my name, and more and more determined to kill the anorectic that was bringing this scourge upon me, this constant interference. As far as these others are concerned, they and the doctor – and the irritation of my name – were the ones to cure me of anorexia, but I have to tell you now – and only you, because you're my friend and have known me for years, that there was never any cure for my anorexic self; I killed the anorectic, as I've already told you, I swallowed it down so that it was no longer visible, no longer on show. No one ever tells you this, but anorexia cannot be cured, only killed and then swallowed – saying all this to Raf, even though I had no idea what I meant by these words 'killed' or 'swallowed', I couldn't help thinking as I ran across the gap at Wattle Street with one or two others, thrilled to be *dicing with death* in this way. Of course, Pamela wouldn't have seen any of this, I had then told Raf as I worked at the prawns, the slime behind their heads – regretting my choice of prawns on such a day and at *such a time in my life*, as I was already fashioning the moment of my breakthrough in my head. By getting to know me then, right at the end of my anorexia, at university, you only got to know me at the time when I'd begun to have nothing more to do with Sarah or her family – for no specific reason or, should I say, for a whole host of reasons. What is familiar to you, then, would be unknown to Pamela and her family; the anorectic that I was and then throttled, if known to them, could only have been known to them from hearsay, I had said, enjoying saying this word 'throttled' to my friend Raf for yet another time that evening, as I recalled now on the pedestrian island near the Moreton Bay fig that had covered the old-boarded up loo in the ivy with its mouldering fruit and the shit from the bats that hung from its branches – the Moreton Bay fig with its oddly small leaves at the far end of the blind and narrow building – and the *other* tree, the tree at *this end*, that I have always thought to be a Moreton Bay fig until now, this close, where it seems a far more European kind of tree – the kind of tree, with its ridged bark and softer, lighter leaves, that would never send roots from the crooks of its branches to suck at the dark hidden things at its base but would rather, as I imagine, lift upwards, as trees are supposed to do. I have no way of knowing, though, if it was the anorectic I had once been that Pamela was smirking at when she smirked at me at the wake – the anorectic via my name or my name via the anorectic – or the name and my connection to it and the largeness of her sister Sarah, as she was trying to describe it. There was, of course, no way, too, that I was going to ask her anything that might clear this up. Pamela has always been an interferer, I had then gone on to say in definite tones, as a way of leading Raf towards another rant I wanted to make – another whose anticipation had already brought heat to my cheeks and the usual numbed, even trembling, incompetence to my lips and my words. Try picturing an interferer and you are picturing Pamela. Even the fact that she first had to point out that her sister had become large should prove it to you – and her words, not just large, but *quite a lot larger*. Those were her words, her very own words. It was off of her to say such a thing at her own sister's wake, with her two younger kids running around behind us, stuffing their faces with the cakes and biscuits that their grandmother had placed on elegant early sixties modernist plates for the adults and not for the children, who only pig out because they are always denied – people who are parents never notice such things. All the time she'd been talking, she'd been leaning against a bench in the open-plan kitchen on which several photos of her sister among vases of yellow and white, too over-petalled flowers had been placed in such a way that the top halves of the photos were shadowed by the hideous bouquets. Pamela seemed to know that she had been off with that statement, or at least off with her smirk about my name, because she then started to fuss about the placement of the photos – pulling some of them forwards and pushing others back – and telling me, rather inconsistently I thought at the time, as I was telling Raf, about how unkind cameras had always been to her sister and how, over the years, they had been conscious to try not to exclude her from family photos and events, but, as I could see, the only photos of her sister showed her off to one side and usually sullen and alone, which was not how she was but only how she came across. They had all shared so much together. She was such a beautiful person, Pamela had said, and it was her statement that they had all shared so much together that triggered something for me: the very imprecision of this word *shared*, and the phrase, *shared so much together* (and coupled with that obvious lie, I'd told Raf: *such a beautiful person*) – this combination of dreadful words that triggered – no, skewered something in the dark at the back of my mind.

You see, all this time since I had first heard the news about the death and the funeral, I remember saying to him – from the phone call I got early on in the week, to the funeral and then the wake – I had no more thought of this sister as being anything more than the dim, unformed image of a sister I had had in the early days of my friendship with Sarah: she was neither kid as we were, nor parent nor teacher. I'd hardly ever seen this sister of Sarah's. In fact I had no memory, or so I thought, of even once talking to her in the past and the pictures in my head of how she had been were particular stills: an anonymous figure in a skirt that was associated with guinea pigs (although the guinea pigs were Sarah's, probably), some high, cork-soled platform shoes by the back door, one on its side, its worn, blue instep facing outwards, a bra with grubby, unlikely conical cups on a bathroom door handle: the archetypal sister. Pamela was the grown-up sister we might always have wanted to have or to be for ourselves. The brother – was he called Doug? Ben? I can never remember – had always been there: as a sharp, foetid smell, or the half-opened door of an inhabited room from which, occasionally, I would hear delicate, plucking sounds that must have been issuing from an acoustic guitar, his own perhaps. But the sister was less than a presence. She was too abstract for that. I'd had a sense she was tall, but this was possibly only because she was six years older than we were, and yet I also had a sense she was real as a person in the way that neither Sarah nor I could ever be real – we were still becoming persons but as kids we had excuses not to be full persons yet: we had the luxury of knowing that we were as yet unformed, as the teachers always said – but Pamela was already the full thing; she was a person, a person who was real and complete in the way we were not, and yet shimmery as a figure: so vague as a figure, and yet infinitely real – as for instance that time I thought I saw her getting out of a car one evening when I was around the side of their house, and a hand with a wrist so hairy that it caught what was left of the sun in the gully into a delicate, wiry aureole – this hand reached out from the side of the car to grab at her burgeoning hip as if only at a cushion that it needed, and the sound that she made was so deep, so surprising, so much halfway between a choke and a very thick laugh that I pressed myself back into the clammy red skin of the bricks in furious embarrassment, hoping that no one had noticed that I was standing nearby, not sure of what I had seen or why it had disturbed me so much. In fact, now that I come to think of it, as I was saying to Raf, washing my hands so that I could top up our glasses with bubbly without smearing them with prawny filth, I can understand that despite all our concrete solidity – at least my concrete solidity – there was a contingency to being as Sarah and I were then, as schoolfriends, as kids who rode bikes around streets and the real, solid houses that vague but real people owned, who went to films that Sarah's parents chose for us and sailed round and around on paid-for skates on a paid-for ice-rink, round and around for no reason at all; who didn't yet list our preferences or even our dreams, so unformed we still thought ourselves, or at least so unformed I thought myself, in my thick child-adolescent body. The more I try to remember what it was that Sarah and I did together or what we said to each other, the less I can remember. I can recall how she talked, but nothing that she said; I remember how I thought, but nothing brought to speech. My whole friendship with Sarah as a teenager is a mystery, and yet I am aware that it took up much of my time both at school and on the weekends, and when I think of Sarah – whenever I try to think of Sarah in any form whatsoever – as an adolescent, as an adult – she is always just something that I see now and then out the corner of my eye: something in her lounge room, by her upright Kawai piano, her tanned legs on the seat; something who was known to inhabit the yellow and blue room that was next to her brother's, and was known to have fought with him often, as someone had told me. But as for any connection between the sister and me, there can be nothing at all but the representation of a connection; compared to my connection with Sarah, which is tenuous but real, my connection with her sister is abstract at the most. If it had only been she and I at the funeral or the wake, or she and I alone during any instance of this time that post-dates the news of Sarah having died, we could only have spoken as one representing family and the present might speak to another representing friends and the past. Anything we should have had to say to each other would have been as one abstraction to another, through the assistance of these supposed but useful designations. I could have expressed my condolences as someone who had once been a friend of her sister's would express her condolences and she, to me, could have expressed her acceptance of these to someone with whom otherwise she would have had nothing to say. But instead of speaking to me as one abstraction to another, this woman who turned out to be so much shorter than I expected her to be and in no way correlated to the image I had when she had spoken to me over the phone or whenever I tried to think of her as the sister – this woman had leaned forwards towards me at the door of the chapel and then later when I arrived at her parents' house for the wake, both times hugging me close as if it had been I and not she that needed the comforting, and, in her smooth but effusive, perfumed banality so essentially unlike the person I thought I had heard so many years ago near her house that I could only doubt the capacity of my memory to keep hold of anything that was true. I was struck so much by the tears in her eyes at the funeral – at the door of the chapel – and then afterwards at the wake, so struck by these tears, which could only have been crocodile tears – just crocodile tears, they were, I'd told Raf, after the cold, even cruelly selfish way she had spoken on the phone a couple of days earlier. After all, she had rung me out of the blue at work of all places to tell me about the death of her sister: her voice then wooden or mechanical, it could have been described – tired, even resentful – this necessity of having to get through a list of people, a very long list, quite likely, of family and friends, to tell all that we needed to know in the shortest possible time; telling it over and over, each time beginning from when someone from Sarah's workplace had rung and her brother gone around, etcetera; from the sound of it, this telling it all, over and over, having already become a huge, an enormous burden – this ringing of people and the speaking rather than anything about the death itself. She didn't know me and I didn't know her, I had thought. I knew Sarah or at least what I remembered to be Sarah but the fact of her death as told by someone I didn't know seemed only to make the fact itself appear as an invention of fact; I listened to the account of the death, the seemingly invented but also medically attested fact of the death – the finding of the body, which in itself was proof, as you would think – but because of the effort that I heard in the telling and because I had no image of this person who was talking to me – no image at all, unless it was the vaguest, as I said, of anonymous figures – a sense of a towering young woman – an adult – in a skirt, but no memory of the adult herself and nor of the skirt in fact – I found myself trying to be kind to this woman who had been burdened with the necessity of ringing; all my attention focused on being kind to this woman – saying exactly what I thought she wanted to hear, this woman who was telephoning me to tell me about the death, the sudden death, of her younger sister, whose death it was obviously difficult to describe, even the necessary details of what she needed to say seeming to take all of her energy and all of her patience; I was so concerned, as I had said to Raf in my kitchen, to attempt to assuage what appeared to be an overwhelming burden, this burden of having to tell – where she spared me neither the deliberations of the work colleagues who hadn't seen or heard from her sister in a couple of days, nor the many attempts on the part of her brother to force open the door of their sister's room in that house in Surry Hills, this door which hadn't been locked, as it was first assumed, but only jammed in that position by the body itself – that it wasn't until afterwards, when I'd put down the phone, that I realised how very smarmy I must have sounded when I'd been talking to her – so much more concerned for saying all the right kinds of things, for soothing a voice whose owner I didn't know, or so I thought

– so much more concerned for this voice than for the death of the friend that was the content of what the voice had been trying to say – and yet this exchange – our exchange over the phone, with neither of us being able to see the face of the other – this exchange, as I said, was at least an exchange, and as I drove off to work that morning, I even had that close, snug feeling, as if I had been someone who had done a good deed. I'd felt as if I had said the right kind of thing in the right kind of soothing tones to someone so worn, so cold, so irritable, that they needed to have these soothing tones communicated to them over the phone. It had all been so abstract, I remember thinking, I'd told him, and Pamela the most abstract of sisters, the most abstract of older sisters – tired, even weary perhaps, but detached, never to be swayed: the kind of sister you might imagine for someone: the kind of sister that everyone has or should have for themselves.

Of course, I should have known straightaway that I knew this sister for herself and not just as a sister, but it took some time for me to realise this. I had thought of her as this abstract kind of sister – of the sort that other people have, and of whom I have always been envious – so competent in the world, so eminently down to earth these sisters are to people like me who don't have sisters. All my life I have wanted to have such a sister, and this is probably what had blinded me to who she was and what she had done to me in the past. I have always been envious of people whose sisters seem to stand for everything that they have been unable or unwilling to attain for themselves – as if these sisters, in their competence, made up for the domestic or romantic shortfalls of their siblings; no one has ever made up for my own domestic or romantic shortfalls. It's pathetic that at my age I still think in this way, but that is how I see it, I had said to Raf, who had only laughed. But when Pamela had said how much she and her family and Sarah had shared together, it had all come back to me then – the deceit of the warmth of these words 'shared' and 'together', plus the deceit of their meaning more than nothing at all. I had heard her say these words 'shared' and 'together' before – as well as 'beautiful person', or not so much heard her say these words but these words being the subject had said themselves, these words in the precise form that they have always said themselves out of Pamela's mouth – the words more important in this case, being the subject, and Pamela the condition – words that, in their utterance, had hounded me once, I then realised, as I had told Raf in my kitchen last night, remembering all of a sudden as Pamela was speaking how I had been enjoined, as it was put in *that place*, that supposed house party, to share as others were sharing – we invite you to share with us, these words had said: *dear Lord* (their tone now rising very slightly, as I then demonstrated), *we just ask that you help us to share together and we just want to thank you that you have brought us together today and we pray for our beautiful sister Jenny. We ask that you enter her heart* – the intoxication of these words, as I remember them, their deliberate but lazy seduction – these words hounding me, chasing me one after the other, through the condition of Pamela, not so much Pamela as she was at the funeral as the Pamela that suggested herself to me through the stirring of those words that I must have heard, for the first time, at a house party that she had asked me to, either by herself or through her sister Sarah, as a deliberate tactic, a gambling with the thing that everyone there at this supposed house party had called my eternal soul.

And so it was, at the wake, that I remembered the *house party*. I should have been remembering Sarah but all I could think about then was the house party that she must have invited me to during my last year at school – inviting me as a friend, no doubt at the instigation of the sister. I had no memory of being invited by Pamela, so I had to have been invited by Sarah, I remember telling Raf yesterday, I thought, as I looked over the collection of second-hand furniture and oddments outside the shop on the north end of Wattle Street, looking at each of the pieces with such care that anyone nearby might have thought that I loved these dusty cane curves and lugubrious glazes. And yet, as I said to Raf, as soon as I tried to think of Sarah at the house party all thoughts of her fell away. Even Pamela fell away when I thought of the house party. Pamela was there because I recognised the words that came out of her mouth and something of the tone, but Sarah must have slipped away from the house party – either deciding not to come at the last minute or going home some time during the weekend. Far from thinking of people when I thought about the house party at the wake, I found that what came to me first, as I thought about it, was a certain state of mind, and that mind in a landscape, a setting, with the words 'house party' spread over everything: this bizarre and inexplicable term 'house party', which I hadn't thought about in years. I was looking at the vases of flowers in the parents' place as I was remembering all this, or more specifically at the shadowing of the flowers over the photos and the top of the kitchen bench, and behind it, at an arched chrome-plated tap that was reflecting distortions of what could have been people in the dining area; and along with the words I was still hearing in my ears even when Pamela had turned away from me for the moment and was talking to someone else behind who was taking a wide tray out of the oven, I kept thinking about the way this term 'house party' spread over a landscape, over a setting and, as it happened, a sombre, sheltered setting: dark-leafed bushes, windows mostly obscured from the outside by the bushes, a path curving round, possibly of concrete, heavily overshadowed, and with one of those low, white skies from an agitated summer already growing prematurely dark – white and yet dark, an indeterminate time of day that was oppressed by the weather. It was called a house party, I had said to my good friend Raf, knowing he had no experience of this, no experience at all, as I'd thought to my pleasure – it was called a house party but there were no houses anywhere that anyone could see, just cabins of the most depressing and flimsy kind: cabins made of some cheap board material that gave no insulating protection during the fierce, dulled heat of the day, and nor any during the bitter and surprising chill of the night. When I tried at the wake to bring to the surface of my mind any more detailed memory or direct impression of being at the house party, all I could bring to the surface of my mind was this indeterminate time of day and the dark, leafy setting – leafy, but when I actually thought of the leaves themselves, a crackling kind of leafiness, where the leaves were neither pliable nor healthy but brown and dry or, if still green, that deep, nearly black shade of green that was dusted underneath, on either side of the stem, on the pale underside of the blackish green, by a sooty mould that came off on your fingers as soon as you touched it. That this path, these windows and the sooty-leafed setting were also in a gully, as was my own house and Sarah's, seemed to go without saying, I had told him, but whether this was because the house party was in a gully – actually situated in a bush gully on the outskirts of Sydney or in the Blue Mountains, as I imagine it, or only seemed to be situated in a gully through association with Sarah and her family, whose house had emerged from a cleft in a gully which ran, or so I remember, only streets away from where I used to live with my family somewhat further down. It's probably not surprising, too, given the setting that I remember, that the state of mind I recall when I try to remember the house party is also agitated and unclear, and, therefore, darker than it might have been, but this setting is important if you want to try to understand what the house party was about, at least from my perspective, as there was a decision that I had been pressed to make at that house party; I had learned, in this setting, that everyone in the world had this decision to make – that everyone who is born into the world has to make this decision and that God would know if the opportunity has come and whether or not it has been wasted; that the fact that I had agreed to come on the house party at the behest of someone or other – either Sarah or her sister – only made the moment of being faced with the decision come sooner to me than it might have come otherwise; that this decision could never be evaded; that I might have felt as if I had been pressed into this seemingly difficult position at the house party, but this was just the opportunity arising as it would have arisen one day of its own accord – if not right then, at the house party with Pamela, then sooner or later, some time before I died, and any attempt to evade this opportunity would be noted by God and tallied against me at the end of all things. *I could say yes to God*, as I had learned at the house party, or I could say no. *I could say yes to God and eternal life or say no to God and be eternally damned.* It was a simple decision. It was all there in the Bible – a Bible that had been handed down through generations of believers, with the words as clear as they could be clear to anyone with intelligence to see, and all of it the Word of God (and the Word was God, as they had said on any number of occasions). I had to say yes to God or no to God and God Himself would judge that my time to decide had come and gone, and so if I did not say yes to God in this instance, it would be read, or understood by God, as no and my fate the same as if I had said no and no and no to God – there not being anything worse, or so I learned during that house party, than the consequences of saying no to God. I could kill whomsoever I liked, I could smear blood from one end of a street to the other – the blood of children and cats and elderly, frail and helpless creatures – and I could say no to God, and each of the instances of murder would mean the same in the eyes of God – the murder and the rejection – or so I had been led to believe, as I'd told my friend as we sat with the prawns only halfway done on my kitchen bench – remembering all this as I waited at the lights opposite a derelict-looking pub I usually hardly noticed, near the beginning of a huge and abandoned work site where there had been a brewery – a once operational brewery, which had been torn down to make way for a development that will reflect, as I had read somewhere, *the most recent thinking and cutting-edge technology in the fast-evolving sustainability industry*. I am in an impossible position, I even remember realising in that setting with the concrete paths and the sooty leaves, I had told Raf. It was clear then and has been clear ever since that the position I'd been put in was impossible and false, and yet thoughts such as these are never allowed to be voiced during events like that house party, unless to be smilingly indulged and then smilingly dismissed. Thoughts that might attempt to be clear at such times and resist the indulgent smiles are considered dangerous and evil, as I had learned at the house party. Satan leads our thoughts if they are clear and unnerving – if they are clear and unnerving, this is proof enough of Satan at work – the snake from the tree of knowledge that slithers into our minds through the gap that Eve opened up (if your mind is open, someone had said, your brains will fall out). God's thoughts are the true thoughts that we should think, I had learned – God's thoughts as they are known, as they are written in the Bible – and yet were written by people, they have to admit, but people who were pure in God the Spirit, the words *of* this Spirit *and so can be tested by love*. Even then, at that house party, I knew I was in an impossible position, and yet I could not do or say anything at that house party without whatever I did or said being interpreted as either a yes or a no to the God that directed the Bible or was said to have directed the Bible, the words being His, somehow, in miraculous English form, in a deadening English that always put me in a dulled, flattened state whenever it was intoned during the kinds of events that they were calling then *quiet times* and *prayer*. I don't remember the people as individuals at the house party at all, I had told my friend Raf as I got him to stand up and help me with the cast-iron wok that was too difficult for me to get down on my own from the shelf above the stove. All this I was recalling now as the pulsing of the signal to walk grew faint as I walked away from the corner, and then louder again as I got closer to the other side of Broadway, and as I walked up the slope towards the huge open sore, the demolished brewery, the locus of innumerable investment hopes (which is how I've described it on many occasions, and as Raf used to call it in his pseudo-professionalese) – my eyes half shut as much to blot out the new low pre-fabricated building that I hadn't expected to see on the site (with what looked to be the word Park across the front of it, the incongruent word Park), as to filter the grit and the dust that my feet were already stirring from the asphalt beneath me (or as I was imagining my feet to be stirring beneath me while I got closer and closer to this Park that certainly wasn't a park just then). I am sure that Pamela was there, and with a boyfriend – a fiancé, I now remember, with a gold band winking between the hairs on a right-hand finger – all of the people at the house party speaking with a slow, drawling ease when they spoke to me and smiling with what looked to be an infinite confidence – all of these fortunate, God-blessed people: kids grown to persons and with boyfriends or fiancés that I nearly admired – all aware, all of them, of being on show as *witnesses*, as they were calling themselves, and satisfied to be thus on show in their hazed and glorious states, but I remember the thoughts rather than the people – my thoughts about the way they spoke, their seeming satisfaction (their triumphant satisfaction) – and the setting of the thoughts: the thoughts and the substance of the setting and so the people, now, without any substance at all, as I had told my friend Raf who had always been immensely curious, as he said in my kitchen, how anyone in their right mind could succumb to this crap. I had been told, I said, that *love was paramount* – not quite understanding this word love as it had been used, but that love was paramount – and that, to these still unknown people, I should pour forth this love in proof of my belief: to let all of the desperate but smiling men without mates left behind by Pamela and her friends – these desperate men, as I remember, not admirable like the boyfriends or fiancés that were already taken by people such as Pamela but desperate and repulsive to the ends of their fingers – their desperate God-given desires wishing only to crawl their hands over my soul. I had to let them crawl their hands over my soul: that is what I remember realising in that house party setting; I had to give up my self to these men because it was what God was asking of me and they, the *witnesses*, silently hoping for. This was the decision I had to make. A horrible decision, and disguised by the idea of love being paramount and that God *just really wanted this for me because I was beautiful*, and the look of the boyfriend/fiancé Pamela had then: his confident smile, his generous, attempting-to-be-a-movie-star ease, his shirt unbuttoned to the third one down, his chest hair on show very chastely, like a ferny corsage: these words *just really* giving a sinister force to everything I learned and was enjoined to believe.

I remember walking down that path – either walking or running; I could have been flying, hovering, even moving as air does – the word 'walking' being nothing but an assumption. There was the path and the windows and the dark, sooty leaves; I passed by and through them as if I had no body, only thoughts that could see and move without effort past the bushes, the windows – weightless – but it was also as if I was hounded, I had enjoyed telling Raf yesterday. I was now thinking about this word once again as I walked up the slope past the no-coloured boarding of this so-named Park: hounded, as in a state of being hounded, I'd said, but with nothing following behind me nor above me nor anywhere near me. In Pamela's parents' house for the wake, then, I kept thinking about that setting: the bushes, the path, the windows with shadows that swallowed all reflections and made ink-coloured pools along the sides behind the bushes and then the dark funnel- ling down through the centre of it all, gradually, the white, white dark of the evening that was fast becoming darker, and it was only by thinking about it in this way, I had then told Raf, that I could begin to make any sense of how those religious ideas had settled in me – ideas that could no more be avoided, as I see it now, than I could have avoided the falling of the dark that was either in my memory or in fact in the setting itself, in the leaves and the dirt; I walked along the path at that house party, ran or floated, disembodied along that path the entire time of the house party as it seemed, but the longer I did so, if in fact I did so, the surer it was that the ideas that had emerged from the house party, the setting of the house party, would settle in the innermost crevices of my mind, to be inaccessible to anything else but the fine, fine dark of the ideas themselves; and so what had seemed clear, I had realised as I tried to explain the thoughts which I could still remember in part from the house party, but only as feelings, as movements of my mind, were now seeming anything but clear, and I remember that even as I talked to my friend Raf last night, I could see I was beginning to doubt what I was saying about my actual thoughts, although I knew I was also trying to be as clear and as honest as

I could with him about the confusion – the clogging of my mind
with the dark – and just as, at that house party, I had been made
to learn that I should always doubt any thoughts that couldn't say
yes and couldn't say no – those thoughts that might only have
been a consequence of those particular bushes and the path, no
more and no less – thoughts which, as I remember – and as I tried
to evoke for my friend when I described the sensations, the physiological and psychological sensations of my *religious conversion*, as
I called it yesterday – were confused, certainly taken aback, by the
necessity of a crisis that had to do with this figment called God – a
crisis I couldn't avoid, no matter how long I lived or wherever I
went, or so said the words that had come from the dusty leaves
of the setting and from the condition of Pamela and her friends;
a crisis that struggled to resist the very idea of the necessity and
supposed inevitability of a crisis – thoughts that in this struggle
had softened, loosened, and thickened into a new substance,
creating the very crevices in my brain for those ideas to settle in an
inverse form – thoughts that were now completely unintelligible,
but that had lodged and taken form from these crevices in my
brain, as I had tried to explain to Raf – thoughts, I could see now
as I walked towards the café and Pamela – my very thoughts at
that 'house party' – that if such a crisis is *meant to be*, it could
also follow that in rising to this crisis, and being proven by this
crisis, my self might find its ultimate self, its ultimate expression
of self – *as God means me to be in His sight* – and so by believing
in God, came my reasoning, through this ultimate decision, I can
also become the great writer that my father is destined never to be,
no matter that he has striven all his life, doing nothing but write
and continuing to fail to write what he wants to write – and now
all the more in his years of retirement, in these many long years
of fighting off cancer: the striving all the more, the failure all the
more – since I, unlike him, or so I must have reasoned at the house
party, have this choice for my choosing (so long as I have the wits
to know it), the choice *to say yes to God* now that my chance has
come, which my father must either never have recognised or never

have taken – a sudden realisation about the ugly and certainly unidealistic reasons for my conversion – about the selfish, calculating, and definitely self-deluding motive behind my supposed conversion – this one sharp wish that must have opened me up, finally, to the falling of the dark and mouldering ideas into my brain – this realisation about my extraordinarily megalomaniacal grounds for converting to God that, catching me as I was walking towards the bus station and Central tunnel in Broadway, was so disturbing, so confronting to my self, that I recoiled from it the moment I thought it – a recoiling that might have looked to everyone on the footpath around me as nothing more than a sudden crumpling or, at best, a sneeze – and so I hurried all the more along Broadway towards the intersection at Regent Street, with the pub and the building that I've always thought looked like an icing-covered building – a building that has been smothered in a sweetness and determined opacity – forcing myself to walk much faster than I would normally be able to – with the dust from the ex-brewery site rasping my throat as I imagined it should, or at least as I was hoping it could (dust being far, far easier to metabolise than stupidity).

A grand, magnificent belief is always selfish, I decided then on my way to Pamela, saying this out loud but through my teeth as I walked past the last of the brewery site, the Art Deco gates that were obviously being kept for *local colour*, as I noticed in passing: don't worry, this kind of noble, very solemn belief is always selfish, I could well have told Sarah had she been coming the opposite way down the street as she had in Rockdale that day, just to reassure her that this supposedly great belief that had occurred in me at that time – occurring as if given by something from without, from above, as they say – this belief that had sliced through the connection between us was less than impure – was laughable, even. I noticed, then, as I was walking and thinking of the possibility of seeing Sarah, that I'd been imagining this possibility everywhere that I'd been outside my flat in the past several days – not so much seeing Sarah as a figure, as herself, but only the shadow of the thought that I might be able to see her – the Sarah as she used to be when we were at school, rather than the Sarah that I had avoided for most of the years that followed and who had obviously not been living very far away from me at all – and so I made this state-ment about belief – a grand, magnificent belief – to myself as I might have said it to *her*, so that the statement might be absorbed by the great wide nought of her habitual silence or else her short and usually tangential replies – so tangential, in fact, they were never replies at all. The act of believing is a selfish one, I muttered, as I would like to have muttered to Sarah, no matter that it was far too late to talk to her. I wanted to be a writer and in order to do this I'd had to renounce everything else; I'd made a deal with God – a deal that I had worked so it was entirely beneficial to my inter-ests; it was weighted towards me (I have to face this, I told myself – just keep remembering your self-justifications, and you might have a chance of facing this) – because I'd said to this God: I will believe in You so long as You make me a great, a famous writer, which surely only You have in Your power to confer – and so, of course, it suited me to keep to this deal, to hold up, to hold on to the conversion that everybody, to their *greatest joy*, as they had told me, witnessed that evening at the house party – the news of my religious conversion rippling outwards in the *fellowship as glad and joyous tidings (oh Lord we really give you thanks that you have really shown Jenny who You are and that she has opened up her heart to You in Jesus' name Amen). This was all that this grand belief was to me, Sarah,* I muttered now, as I would like to have said to my one-time friend – this ridiculous situation of my brain, this scrambling of thoughts into the word belief, into this clichéd approximation of a conversion that was, in fact, my own sort of conversion, both the cliché and my selfish misreading becoming one large dreadful occasion – the celebrated *conversion of Jenny at the house party* – even as the offering of these thoughts to the impossible figment of a resurrected Sarah is just an excuse, I told myself as I walked away from the brewery site, this Park that wasn't yet a park: this imag-ining that I might even be able to excuse myself from all those years that I had ignored (and in fact avoided) Sarah, even though I also remember the relief that I'd felt, after the house party – the relief of being shielded from the *intensity of tedious Sarah*, as I had once put it to a schoolfriend – shielded from Sarah, I was thinking as I continued walking away from the Park and towards the icing-covered building, by the luxury of this grand and noble conversion that gave me a reason for a time, so long as I held on to the terms of the conversion, to keep away from unbelievers *for the sake of fellowship with God*, my renunciation being little more than what I might have done, I thought as I ran across Regent Street while a single small blue car seemed to burn up the lane towards me, if I had emptied all my worldly possessions onto the Black Jack table at the casino that was yet to be built in Sydney, hoping to win not only the triple of my bet that evening but also the sure demeanour of the glamorous men and women who would be dealing out the cards – their collective glamorous demeanour. Believing in this kind of belief, I could have said to my old friend Sarah – believing in this kind of belief is also an indulgence in vertigo: the belief as a sugary giving-in to the melodrama of a fall, a jump into the idea of jumping into nothing (but only the nothing that someone else has already described). All right, I could well have said to her, I then mumbled as I passed the small shop that sold bus tickets and articulated umbrella guards, I had been lured into the thrall of a grand belief – and it was a mind-spinning headiness, a wide, smug feeling of falling into a fragrant void – a breathlessness, a readiness for something great that I'd always wanted and always hoped could be mine – and this is the ambience that you have evoked for me in that manuscript you wrote and left behind you, *Panthers and the Museum of Fire*, because there is something in it, something, which must have reminded me on Saturday, if not of the grand belief itself, which was remote then, unbelievable even – and confined to a time that has long ago passed – but of the moments that immediately followed it: that sweet, sweet falling into something large. I remember this declaration of belief: I remember becoming conscious that I was believing at last – that now, after a grand *inner journey*, I had found myself within the fold, as they'd put it – the significance of *the fold*; I remember the euphoria of believing that, with belief, I had become the protagonist of a story – and not just any story: *the only one there is.* I remember the euphoria of this belief in myself as protagonist – which must always have been part of my grand, my magnificent moment, I was thinking as I walked through the people grouped at the bus stops towards the slope that headed down to the tunnel under the railway lines, this euphoria that was not just an associated feeling, but, in fact, very likely, the significant thing itself. And there was also the relief – the thought that the role of protagonist was mine at last, and that it had not been allowed to pass me by – that there had been something in me, a power that had always been there, very hidden, in my self – a rare and noble, intrinsic quality that had enabled me to reach out to grab this belief for my self at the house party – I remember the grateful conviction that I'd actually had the foresight and wisdom and laudable strength to grab at the belief as it was offered and hence I had not consigned my self to insignificance as so many others had done in the world (*many are called but few are chosen*). This is what it feels like to be one of the elect, I remember saying to myself. And so, even though the belief in the God of the house party has long been unbelievable – since all those years ago when I had struggled to extricate myself first from Pamela's church and then the church of her friends, from the company of people who believed that they had my soul in their hands after what I had said or was supposed to have said at the house party – even though I have put all this behind me, as it were – this welling of belief in my self as protagonist of a grand and significant story is something that pulls at me still. Perhaps it was this secondary, but far more significant, belief that I recalled in the feel of the manuscript as I was reading it, I was thinking as I walked down the tiled concrete slope – this manuscript that Sarah had written rather than I, myself – a manuscript that had everything in it that could ever have been written had it been I rather than Sarah who had sat down to write it – a manuscript of the sort, I could see, that I had bargained my soul away at the house party to have for my self, so to speak, and which had failed to materialise even during those short dense years when I still believed in the God that I'd said I believed in. A manuscript about everything and also about nothing: a hold-all object, as Virginia Woolf says – a manuscript in which everything is possible, everything can be written. A manuscript (now my very own manuscript since my breakthrough, however poor a substitute) whose existence I tend and on whose behalf I worry that all might fail me – my time, my health, my energies – all that I have sacrificed thrice over already but now, like a desperate, unprincipled gambler, must convince once more to be sacrificed again.

And so, yes, it comes down to a manuscript (mine), I told myself as I remembered the way I had described the manuscript (hers) to my good friend Raf: not so much about the manuscript itself but the event of the manuscript, the manuscript that my one-time friend had left behind her, as they say in all famous writers' biographies (like the one for Ern Malley, that ultimate writer of left-behind manuscripts). I'd told Raf how I had not wanted to read the thing – exaggerating my resistance – using gestures that I hadn't even thought to use at the wake, when I was supposedly using them – this manuscript that Pamela had practically foisted on me, I'd said, at the afternoon tea after the funeral because of what she remembered about me and my *literary flair*, as she called it, not letting me leave the house without it, even though I had left the manuscript, to be discreet, under the pile of photograph albums near the telephone in the hall. Somebody gives you something you don't want, I'd told Raf, putting the finished prawns to one side at last, and taking from the fridge a melon that I needed to skin, and you leave it, as if by accident, in a place out of sight, and so you are right to be speechless when the very same thing is returned at the door just as you leave. You are right to be surprised that what you have done has been misinterpreted or brushed aside; that the general words of polite and sympathetic interest that you had given the manuscript the first time, just to be kind, should be repeated in quotation marks as the manuscript in its plastic bag is handed over for the second time, and this second time with even more witnesses nearby to notice what has been said and how it has been said; how all the gestures I recognised from the house party – all those gestures of inclusion, of fellowship, that I remembered – that listening look with the head on the side, the far too positive words, the hand on my upper-arm in a half embrace – should now be used to hound me a second time: the tears in the sister's eyes – less at the death of her sister than at the sensitive, sisterly role that she had played at the funeral and now, above all, here among all these beautiful flowers at the wake.

At the door of the chapel, and later at the wake, I had been so completely taken aback by those tears that coursed down the face of the sister that I probably came across as a much colder person than I actually am, I'd told Raf as we both sat there with the melon that I'd started to skin: Raf waiting to take it from me, as he'd offered, to dice it into chunks. All the way to the crematorium in my car, I had told him, I had still been cocooned in that feeling – that close, snug feeling, as I have described it. That morning I left my flat, content that this time I wasn't driving towards the east side of Sydney, where I work if you remember, but was in fact driving west and then north over the harbour; content that I was taking *special leave*, as it's put, for the funeral of a *very old friend*. I had stiffened for the hugs at the chapel and later at the wake, but until I was talking to Pamela near the photos in the open-plan kitchen I couldn't account for this reaction of mine. Every day since Pamela rang me the first time, I'd told Raf, I had been thinking of Sarah – sometimes addressing myself, or telling one of my friends at work – and all the time referring to her as *a very old friend*. I had known her for years and years, I told all who'd listen: it was now, technically speaking, over two-thirds of my life. The whole of my life spreads before me in wavering indistinctness as I talk like this; as I talk, I can see my life as it stretches its pale yellow light in all directions – a pale yellow light that contains, in patches, remembered impressions of Sarah's face: *my very old friend.* I softened in the telling and retelling of this supposed fact, I'd told Raf as he sat in my own *closed plan* kitchen last night, helping me with the melon (even though over a year ago, I had wanted to remind him but knew I couldn't, his words *your friend* had turned me off wanting to have anything to do with her ever again). All the pictures of Sarah in my head, now that she has died, are dated from the days that she had been at school with me and from no other time, least of all from that day when we met by chance with my printer in Rockdale. Obviously, I had *withdrawn* from my one-time friend as her adult self, I then realised as I walked down the concrete slope towards the tunnel, and so if she had become unimportant and trivial it was even possible that I was the one that had made her that way.

I had said to Raf that nothing I heard in the chapel at the crematorium reminded me of the friend I had once had or explained that friendship. I could see her coffin, of course, and the parents, who I recognised, although they were so much reduced, and the sister that I had only just met for the first time, as I'd thought, and a man who had to be either her brother or her husband – a thickened, stiff-backed man with fuzz on his neck – but otherwise there was nothing at all that connected me with Sarah. An obscene-looking man had spoken at the funeral, speaking of Sarah, but nothing that he said triggered any kind of memory that I might have had of her. He talked about Sarah's value as a daughter and a sister. He talked about her work at the council and where she had lived. He talked about her travels in Japan and quoted from some emails that she had sent her family from there: banal emails with plenty of clichés about family and friends that he must either have written himself or fished with care from a gigantic trawl. He finished with a pompous introduction to a song whose chorus went: *Nothing compares to you* – supposedly her favourite song, as he had said – although how on earth he could have known it was her favourite song, I remember thinking at the time, I'd told Raf – even if he was the brother or the brother-in-law or just a minister, it didn't matter – how on earth could he have known such a thing as this unless someone had told him? People are always passing on supposed facts about somebody else – supposed facts about favourite foods and songs and books – and most of the time they are completely wrong. Just because someone had once said they liked a certain song or a certain book or a certain drink, you can be sure that someone else will remember this person saying that this song, this book or this drink was their favourite thing in the world. Perhaps all it takes is for you to hum the tune of a chorus one day for no other reason than someone else in the bus had been humming that tune or that you thought you'd heard it emerging in the tinsel vibrations from their ear buds, and everyone in the office that day begins to surmise that this tune that they recognise too is the song that best defines you, that they could call your favourite song when anybody asks them should it turn out that you die that week or a short time later. How many times is it that you hear something that you've said being turned against you in this way: some reckless comment, some off-the-cuff remark, some coincidence in ordering, say, a blueberry frappé two times in a row with the same group of people. Beware where you walk, beware what you say, I'd said to Raf as I measured the rice into a saucepan. You can even tell a story in one way just to hear it come back to you told, as if you'd told it, in another way entirely. Time and time again this has happened to me. Even those extracts from the emails at the funeral, I'd said, and the conclusions that the man had drawn about Sarah's life from those short few lines in the emails: perhaps she had written those words one after another in that particular order but what else had she written in that email, let alone in the next, and what else had she thought, either during the writing of that email or immediately afterwards? How many times do we press the send button only to regret in an instant the wording: have I been too gushy, too romantic, too heartless, too irritable, too spare, too niggardly, too pedantic, too self-satisfied, too fey? If so: too late to send a correction or a retraction. What kind of an obsessive sends a correction? And even with Facebook, I had said to him, since I knew Raf always liked to hear my rants against Facebook – and all those sites like Facebook, where you can at last describe yourself as your self, your essential self – where you can list all your favourite songs and links, display all your friends, or at least the images that your friends or supposed friends have put up – how can we be sure that what we put up today we will like tomorrow when it's already been seen – and, indeed, what if we *accidentally* like a post or an image, clicking on the *like* button when we meant to click on *play*, and having to leave this *accidental like* on the glowing screen of the worldwide web, because isn't it far, far worse to *unlike* it afterwards? How can we know we are even in our right mind when we say or click that we like this song or that song, listing our favourites in searchable links, with each of these favourites presuming to be the very same favourite as the blue-linked wording in another kind of list on another person's site, where neither the one nor the other is recognisable as something familiar, where none of it at all is recognisable (our own site suddenly other, alien, somebody else's – the feeling all wrong)? All this had been going through my head as I listened to the song that they played at the end of the speech · going through in concentrated form, I had told him – until I realised that the coffin had disappeared; that all the time I had been thinking these thoughts, the coffin had either been lowered into the storey below or slid backwards behind the curtains, and either way the process had happened in silence or the sounds of the coffin sliding on tracks or being lowered on cantilevers had been covered over by the song – all the scraping and squeaking of the moving parts smoothed over, even smothered, by the song – a song which I remembered actually liking when it had come out over a decade ago – or not so much liking but finding myself singing over and over – this song which in no way correlated with anything that I could imagine, let alone remember, about my old friend Sarah. No doubt, I then realised at the funeral after the song had finished, as I'd gone on to tell Raf – this thought coming at me suddenly – Sarah has already been burned. They have only played that song to distract us so that we might not notice that the coffin has had to move away, so that the body could be burned and disposed of quickly. There had been several chapels in the crematorium, or so I had noticed when I arrived, all of them pointing inwards like the leaves of a clover to a stalk, and Sarah's wasn't the only memorial service in the crematorium: the chapel next door was already emptying out as we were gathering, and another event, I'd seen, was about to begin. The furnace would have been at the back of the chapel – it was either at the back or directly beneath where we all had been sitting – and the moment the coffin was gone it had probably been burned; there would have been a roar and a flare and a whitening into ash. The song was a ruse then, I'd told my friend Raf as he worked at the melon yesterday, and it was very likely it had never been a favourite song of Sarah's at all, but just the most apt, most covering-over song there was – or the most easily found one: the CD on the top of the pile in the room that the family had just started to clear the day before the funeral, when the director of the service had asked for some *music to smooth the proceedings.*

All the same, there had been nothing I could say to either the family or the friends of the family (there hadn't been any other friends of Sarah's, only friends of the family). If only I could have thought of some short and sensitive phrase to offer in memory of Sarah, I'd said – something that I could have been sure was true as well as appropriate to say – I might have had something to offer as I filed out of the chapel behind everyone else, something more than the meaningless phrase I came up with – some meaningless phrase, which I had overheard someone else using and which exact combination of words I've already forgotten. For some reason I had wanted to comment on the travels in Japan, which I had never heard about and couldn't imagine happening – Sarah who had never seemed to want to go anywhere at all – but I had resisted this compulsion for fear of appearing too surprised or ignorant – after all I was her friend, as I had been told by the shortish middle-aged woman that I soon realised had been Pamela at the door of the chapel the moment I arrived. This woman who had been so grateful that I'd been able to come, since I was the only friend that she knew of, the only one she could ring – it being a sad, sad thing but there had been nobody else.

As I walked back to my car after the service – passing by a section that opened out at the back of the chapels, where I couldn't help noticing a young man in gum boots pulling a filthy-looking wheelbarrow backwards – I kept thinking about this fact that Pamela had told me when I had arrived for the funeral: this supposed fact that I was Sarah's only friend. This wasn't the first time I had got the impression that the family thought in this way, I was realising as I followed the path down the hill to my car after the service, and as I'd told my friend Raf yesterday evening, but as it had been many years since I had seen them – by which I meant the parents, very obviously, not the brother or Pamela – I had forgotten how important I had supposedly once been to Sarah, or, should I say, to her parents instead. Although I cannot remember exactly the first time that the parents had met me during Sarah's first year at my school, I do remember my surprise at how quickly they had latched on to me, the parents treating me as no one had ever treated me before: as if I'd been an ambassador of some sort, some powerful, moneyed friend, when all the time, as they knew so well, I was a nobody from nowhere and it was they who were powerful, they who were rich. Although their house had been a timber and brick multi-levelled place cleaving into the gully in the very same way that my own parents' house had been a timber and brick multi-levelled place cleaving into the very same gully, only much lower down, theirs had had classy light coverings rather than those sad bare bulbs in all the rooms and they'd had a new Mercedes with real leather seats – as well as a smart little Saab that the brother was learning on. We only had an oldish Ford that could never fit into the garage because of the junk your father insists on putting there, as my mother has always said. Sarah's mother wore several gold rings whereas my own mother wore one; Sarah's mother had her hair waved and dyed, the other greyed early; our clothes were all hand-me-downs whereas Sarah's were new. Everything of theirs was always new. Their garden was always tidy, the leaf droppings always swept away by a gardener who came once a week, whereas ours was wild, scabrous, bare and twiggy under trees that had been allowed to grow too big and for far too long, half-dead, and concealed disintegrating cardboard boxes of magazines, books and newspapers that my father had cleared out of the garage once to appease my mother when he was setting up his study in the room under the stairs – this room once called the Rumpus Room, now his Study or Writing Room – so at last he could write the book that would make us millionaires, as he'd yelled when my mother had tried to intervene so she could keep the room sufficiently clear, as she said, of your rubbishy ideas so visitors could at least come down to play table tennis now and then as they did in any normal house – these boxes of crackling, disintegrating paper that he had simply forgotten either to throw away or bring back into the garage or the Study-cum-Rumpus Room which he was still setting up, even now at seventy-nine, he is still setting up – at the very same age, I'd told Raf, as I only learned from my aunt these last several months, that his own mother, who'd been struck mute in her late twenties after she'd been attacked on her way to the butcher's on a busy afternoon by nobody that anyone has ever been able to identify, had suddenly, inexplicably, begun to cry and paw at the people around her – my father spending the entire remnant of his life, as it seems, setting up for the one great work that everyone continues to ridicule him about no matter that he is writing and writing – so very obviously writing every hour of the day. They were the rich ones, the savvy ones – Sarah's father who had arranged his general practice so he could keep his golfing partner happy on Wednesdays, whose whim he could never cross, as he used to joke when I was there with the family during the holiday weeks – how he would touch his wife's arm with the tips of his fingers just as he left the house towards noon and with a comical, mock-eager look, say he was off to a *dire medical emergency*, and each time Sarah's mother would laugh in her murmuring, pleasant way – this joke that, for all I knew, the father might only have continued to say because I was there. They were the rich and witty ones. We were the poor and bereft of anything to say. Although Sarah had had to leave the private school, I had heard – leaving the school her sister had gone through and her mother before her – it hadn't been a question of money. They were still the rich ones; I was still the poor. And yet somehow I would always be the example, the person to look up to whenever one or the other of Sarah's parents needed to refer to someone as an example. Jenny would do this, I would hear from them regularly – particularly the mother; Jenny likes eating her apples with the skin *on*; Jenny wouldn't cut her hair as short as that. Since I didn't have pierced ears then, at the time – not for lack of wanting them, I'd told Raf as I got up at last to fry the prawns so that they would still be warm when the rice was ready, it was simply that my mother wouldn't let me (I would be cheapening myself, I'd become a whore) – since my ears weren't pierced in those days, my smooth, intact earlobes became the example of what was done, or rather not done, in the best, the most high class circles – the very circles in which, I had always thought, that Sarah's family belonged and we never could. It didn't matter that I longed for my ears to be pierced – that I'd had many battles with my mother over this very desire – saying how little I cared that I would look like a prostitute; that even Princess Anne had pierced ears, or the daughter of one of my mother's friends – one of the friends she always referred to. In fact, my opinion would never be sought on the matter (by Sarah's mother), or if so, it would be assumed by a leading question, such as: *You wouldn't have your ears pierced, would you Jenny? You would think it was cheap. You would never wear make-up to school.* And flattered by their confidence in me – even knowing that Sarah must have hated me for saying what I went on to say – I would always agree with them, always concur.

There had really been no reason that I could think of at the time for why I had been held in such esteem, I'd said to my good friend Raf last night while the prawns were sizzling. Nobody had ever held me in such high esteem before and, very likely, will never do so again. All I had been was the friend of the daughter. Here I am,

I remember saying to myself as I was hugged in the doorway at the wake when I arrived, here the friend of Sarah, who has always been welcome – more the friend of the family than a friend of the daughter's – the welcome of the family (via the parents back then) always seeming to be grossly disproportionate to how I felt as a friend of the daughter's – here I am: arrived as requested: the friend of the family who has always been described as a friend of the daughter's; who has always believed herself to be one of many friends or at least acquaintances of the daughter's, by no means the only friend from her years at the local high school, which the family must have resisted having to send her to, let alone the long years and decades afterwards, but who has now been told a second time – this time in front of others – that she is the only one – not the only representative of the friends, the only one who could make it, as she might have believed, but the only friend that Sarah had ever had in all the years she had been alive.

As for the sister herself, she was a stranger to me at first, as I have said, I'd told Raf. Very likely I only represented, for her, one of her sister's many friends from the past, I had thought, not yet willing to believe that what the sister had said could be anything more than an exaggeration. Even she believes the exaggeration for itself, or wants to believe it, I had told myself as I kept very still for that hug in the doorway at the wake, when so many people had been looking on. As I arrived on that faux Tuscan porch with the faux Tuscan urns – the one-level place the parents had retired to in the centre of a group, a whole cemetery of faux Tuscan urns in a retirement village with the absurd name of North Ryde Florentine Views, which I might have been able to imagine the father making jokes about, had I not just seen him further back in the hall reduced to slipping a biscuit into his pocket – I could see how Pamela's eyes were filling with tears as she turned from a woman she was hugging so she could prepare for me, as if it were her house she was welcoming me to, her own faux villa. She only had to see me now in this light – that is, in the light of her exaggeration – for the tears to seep – those tears which shocked me then, the way they oozed down her face as if from a vast infection or allergy – so unprepared I was to see such an emotional display towards me from the person who'd been so cool, even irritable, on the phone – these tears which had so astonished me, I'd told my friend Raf, that I had been unable to do anything but allow myself to be absorbed into the exaggeration she had prepared for me and feeling, in my entrapment, as she hugged me in that doorway for a full five minutes, as someone who, unable to escape in time from a drunkard, covers over her failure to do so by humouring the person.

It was then, I'd said, when I was thus entrapped in front of everyone at the door of the villa, that Pamela told me about how dear I had been to the whole family over the years, saying again how glad she had been that I'd been able to come to the funeral – the only friend of Sarah, which was simply terrible, as she said, allowing herself to he heard – in fact wanting to be heard, the loud, first stressed syllable of this word '*ter*-rible'. It was a *ter*-rible, sad indictment of things that I was the only friend of her sister, the only friend that her sister had ever had, saying this in the full hearing of the others who weic there behind her in the hall. Everything that she said to me at the wake she said in the full hearing of somebody else, both at the door as I arrived, and then afterwards in one of the many rooms, this sister that I didn't know, or so I thought, but understood to represent the sister of the person who had been a friend to me at school, who seemed only to be able to speak to me if she could do so when others could listen to what she had to say. Both at the door of the faux Tuscan villa and later, in one of its various rooms, this sister, Pamela, talked to me or talked to others in my presence, as if what she was saying to them she was also saying to me – and so everything that she said she was obviously wanting me to hear and for others to see that I was hearing. The brother was there, I had heard, as were the parents and other relatives and what had to be the friends of either the brother or the sister or the parents or the relatives, but it was to me that Pamela seemed to want to speak and to be seen to be speaking, and for a while I was utterly at a loss as to why this could be.

It was in the open-plan kitchen that she asked me about my *literary pursuits*, I'd told my friend Raf last night as he laboured over some snake beans for me, and was remembering now as I stood for a moment near the bottom of the tiled concrete slope on the way into Central tunnel, where there is a shoe repair business in the name of a Marcel who always appears in my mind, when I pass it, with dark, hooded eyes and a drooping moustache – who, simply as a name at the entrance to this tiny shop has, for years, looked out at me and smiled – no matter, as I've often told myself, that the real Marcel in his workshop, whom I have never actually wanted to see, has probably ruined his eyesight and his lungs with the stink of leather, vinyl and glue – that he would no doubt think me a raving lunatic for thinking of his name, Marcel, in this comforting way. I remember telling Raf that at first, in the kitchen of that faux Tuscan villa, I'd thought Pamela was only asking me about my *literary pursuits* because of my father. If you have a father who is a writer, even a completely unsuccessful writer as my father has always been – the height of his achievement being his collection of short biographies, *Fame and the Infamous: Noteworthy Inhabitants of Ku-ring-gai Shire,* of which only a hundred were ever printed and twenty-three sold – to the people, no doubt, who either were, or were related to, the people there mentioned – a collection of biographies that he has often cursed, so much has it distracted him from the brilliant work, as he puts it, that's boiling inside him and even though he's written thousands and thousands of pages has yet to be brought to the surface – if you have a father who is a writer of this sort, however misunderstood (his embarrassing distractions taken for achievements, as he has more than once said to me or to anyone listening), it often happens that people will assume that you are a writer, too – or if not a writer, something else *creative*: there is a subgroup of Sydney people that is only interested in the *creative* so long as it might promise an occasion to dress up – fantastic, they will say if you tell them you paint, do you have exhibitions? Can you invite me to your shows? At high school – although Pamela couldn't have realised this, I had been thinking, unless her sister had told her, I had been known for my involvement in the school magazine. I had been the one to craft the journalism of what had been a yearly paper, I was remembering now, as I lingered by the bins opposite Marcel's boot repair shop, but had not wanted to tell Raf – a yearly paper, which, until the moment I began work on it, was little more than the regurgitated formula of school magazines in any high school in the state: the yearly sporting triumphs, the yearly debating outcomes, the yearly bland, cheerful and therefore hopelessly discouraging message from the Principal, the mini biographies of each of the current Year Twelve students, who would be the only people to leaf through the pages, in search of themselves. I had taken this magazine and *taken it somewhere else*, as someone had said of me in my own mini biography at the end of my schooling. I had taken a fairly standard annual paper, with its lists of cross-country champions and Year Twelve anecdotes and turned it, as it was put, into a *far-fetched monthly literary experience*. I had no illusions that the more general reader of this *far-fetched monthly literary experience* would have had any reasons to regret my retirement from the school magazine when I exited the school at the end of Year Twelve. Most of the readers' letters had been nothing but criticisms or jokes. And yet it had been expected that I would go on to *even greater heights* – the metaphor of the distant Nepalese mountain peaks coming naturally to those of my fellow students who would soon be trekking and climbing the physical ones once their first pay packets had arrived. I would, of course, get a training position on one of the city's newspapers. I would write a novel, plays, short stories or at least the kinds of wisecrack observations that might be printed in the famous Column Eight of the *Sydney Morning Herald*. Unbeknownst to Pamela, or so I had to expect, I had been famous for my writing, my far-*fetched* writing, but since the days at high school – during the many days, months and decades that had passed since then – the most far-fetched aspect of my writing was its distance from any kind of success. I had wanted to become a writer. I had spent years and years doing nothing but attempting to write and continuing to fail – the most I had done was to publish a couple of insipid stories in the most obscure and under-read journals in the world, and yet I did not tell this to Pamela as she continued to probe, and neither had I felt like telling Raf last night even though I had relayed to him Pamela's questions about my *literary pursuits*. The more Pamela tried to ask questions of me about my *literary pursuits* the more I realised that she must have heard something of what I had always wanted to do but signally failed to achieve. Perhaps Sarah had once told her something, I had then started to think while I was standing in her parents' kitchen – although I can't imagine Sarah telling her anything – perhaps somebody at the funeral has remembered me from school, although I can't imagine that either, there being nobody here that I recognise and, after all, aren't I the only friend of Sarah here, the only one at all? In the end all I managed was a raising and a twisting forwards of my shoulder. I had no idea what this sister was trying to get at, I'd gone on to tell Raf, so I had raised and twisted my shoulder – the kind of shrug that some might interpret as a gesture of deliberate self-deprecation – which was intended to come across as a gesture of deliberate self-deprecation – the kind of gesture that Australians are known for – even the famous, as I have often said to people at work – and it was across this completely fake and falsely humble gesture that Pamela had pressed me with the manuscript – deliberately misreading something which should have been obvious as a feeble attempt to salvage the unsalvageable, that is my failed literary ambitions, I was thinking now, opposite Marcel's, but had not wanted to disclose to Raf. She had insisted that I have a look at the manuscript, a really good look, I had told Raf in the end, while I tossed the snake beans, some fish sauce, vinegar and sugar in with the prawns, because she has always been sure that something special would come from this beautiful sister of hers.

As I served out our meal in bowls I told Raf that it was only afterwards I realised that all the time she'd been speaking to me about my literary pursuits, she'd had a small, tight smile on her face and a self-conscious look, and that this was probably because she knew I was working at a radio station (after all, she had rung me there) and was therefore *in the arts* as people say – perhaps it was nothing to do with my father (or my *far-fetched* writing in the high school magazine). However she had got my number – from my parents, most likely, who still live near the bottom of the gully, as you know, I'd said – who have failed to move from its inconvenient damp and too numerous levels because everything is so expensive and made of rubbishy materials that all leach cancerous substances, as my father usually puts it – however she had got my number, she must have found out that I worked *in radio*, and it was this idea that she must have known that I worked for a radio station that seemed to account for her manner in talking to me when I thought about it later. I have realised over the years that when people meet someone who works for the media, they are instantly interested, instantly impressed, I had told my friend Raf last night as we began to eat. The fact that all I do is the lowest of the low research for a notorious show that I am usually too mortified to name – that all these years I have continued to do this menial, unintellectual, even embarrassing, work – too lazy I was realising now as I leaned against the wall by the bins near Marcel's, fiddling with my phone so that I would not look too suspicious, but also so that I might keep myself from running too eagerly towards Pamela, like a dog with a chewed-over ball – too lazy and too shy of using up all my supposed writing energy to organise a move to a more worthwhile or interesting section of the station – or to another radio station completely where I know I would work a lot harder for far less pay – the fact that I work in this embarrassing job, spending my time either exaggerating facts or covering them up – feeding rubbish to the presenter who, herself, has even less interest than I do in the truth of the matters I research, interested only in what sensationalising story she can present, what ratings she can scoop and how good she looks in that little red number that Marketing picked out for her press release – the fact that the work I do at the radio station is not only meaningless and useless but a deliberate act of distortion, and whose only positive role in the world, as I have said to you on any number of occasions, is to be a source of anecdotes for people like you – paraphrasing Mr Bennet, as I always have, I'd been thinking as I spoke – this fact would mean nothing to the likes of Pamela, I had said, enjoying being able to call this ranting a *fact*. I have grown used to the kind of self-conscious reaction that I saw in Pamela whenever I meet anyone who discovers, as I am talking to them, that I work in radio. I should have noticed this right from the beginning, but for some reason I didn't. It was the reference to my name, I had then insisted to Raf, it was the reference to her sister being large and the coy but very obvious reference to my name which had thrown me right at the start, not long after I'd arrived at the wake. Why on earth would I then have got on to thinking about my father, I'd asked my friend, since I was not wanting to tell him about my *far-fetched* writing in the high school magazine. Pamela had insisted that I have a look at the manuscript, a really good look, and so I should immediately have known that she had heard from someone that I worked in radio. It was the sort of smile and self-conscious look that is the look of somebody who is readying herself for something, who is attempting to look normal for a microphone or a camera when she can never look normal even without either of those. She reminded me of myself, I had told him, all those years ago when I had first got that in at the radio station, when I was still in awe of the radio station *per se*; when I still thought my life would at last find the course that it was meant to find (when I might, being surrounded by creative, literary minds in the radio station, finally become the brilliant writer that I wanted to be). I was realising that at the time, at the wake, as Pamela was pressing me with the manuscript, I didn't think about my job at the radio station but instead, once I twigged to who she was, could only start to wonder whether she still believed in God as she had done at that house party and for the several years afterwards, when I had seen her now and then *in fellowship circles*. Of course, I wasn't going to ask her such a question. I always dread this kind of question myself. Whenever, over the years, people that I had known at the various churches that I went to after the house party have asked me *which church I go to*, no matter how strongly I feel about the issue – no matter how much I detest that whole culture, as I have put it before, of preying on the sanity of others, of digging its claws into other people's minds – I've found that there has never been a simple response that I can give. It has exhausted me, this needing to excuse myself to people who assume I still believe. No matter how much and how long I have ranted to people like you about belief, I still dread this confrontation with believers – their declared disappointment, their horror, their anger, their fear – or, indeed, their well-founded suspicions. When Pamela had said that she had always been sure something special would come from this sister of hers, I had been thinking that she was going to ask me about my belief – the word 'special' being particularly telling, particularly inviting, but the more she talked, the sooner I realised that she took my belief, any such belief, my supposed belief, entirely for granted. She is assuming that I still go to church as a result of that house party, I thought as she was talking, even though I had left that church as soon as I could, under the pretext of finding a church that was easier for me to get to – Pamela's church being, for some reason, several suburbs away from where both of us lived. People are always assuming that other people's lives are no different from how they had seemed many years earlier, no matter that it has been years and years since they and the others have seen or talked to each other. You look at someone you once knew and you immediately fall to assuming that you know everything that it is possible to know about that person. It is just the fact that this person is recognisable, and, of course, associated with feelings and memories – or supposed feelings and memories – it is just this association that makes us think that we know this person *as she really is*. To Pamela, no doubt, I am still the girl who lived down the road and whom she'd managed, somehow, to get to the house party and *bring to the house of the Lord*, even though her whole simpering attempt at being normal seemed to betray the fact that she also knew that I worked in radio – and therefore that, to her, this girl down the road in the gully has an extra significance: she is just one of us *but she can tell the whole world through her radio work, a triumph for Christians*. They know not a thing about what is happening in your head, but they treat you as if you are still at the mercy of the grand belief they once hounded you into taking on; having preyed on your sanity, just to keep themselves believing – always hounding someone else so they can stay believing – they treat you as if you are still the person they hounded all those years ago, as if their hounding of your mind had not sent you off chasing your fugitive thoughts, but with this addition: to their delight they discover that you work in radio and are therefore *creative*, and it is suddenly as if they themselves had a chance to do something in radio and so in the *creative fields*. You are their investment, still. Whatever you do or can do, *now they can do themselves through you*. No matter that you are a desiccated shell of a person, I might have added to Raf yesterday but didn't – no matter that your life has become one long debacle, as you have never been able to connect to anyone for any length of time – no matter that for years you have imagined what you might have done otherwise, but have at least managed to crawl a long way out of the mire, as far as you can away, so obsessed with getting away you never look forwards – no matter that you're convinced that the distance you have put between you and their belief is the greatest that could ever have been gained, you are still the one they successfully got: a trophy, a prize in their hands, their human soul.

But it was then, I had told my friend Raf as I got up to open the wine that he had brought – which I'd almost forgotten about – it was then, across all the thoughts I was having about her possible belief that this sister, Pamela, began to tell me about how unusual Sarah had always been, and how I was the only person apart from the family ever to realise what this meant. Sarah had never been like any other children, she was saying to me and anyone else in the kitchen (and in the dining room, too – it being an open-plan kitchen as I'd said), and this had made it difficult for Sarah when she tried to mix with others. She never had an easy way with talking to other people, as I no doubt remembered, and this had led teachers, and of course other children, to assume she was arrogant as well as inept. Children are cruel and teachers are cruel. The whole world is cruel to people who don't talk in that easy chatty way that other people do, and so it often follows, said Pamela, that these people are assumed to have nothing worth saying and, worse, are rejected by everyone else, no matter that their mind is brilliant, no matter that they top the state in Maths. This was what had happened to Sarah, and it had happened to Sarah from the very beginning. She had been marked from the start, Pamela had not been shy of saying in front of me and the several others near us in the kitchen – her own friends most likely – as if we were all part of the same little club, I'd told Raf, all with the same thoughts on life and *the way things were*.

She and Sarah, of course, had gone to the same junior school as we knew but she (Pamela) had left before Sarah began, and so it was clear to her what was happening to her sister. She was no longer in the thick of the junior school herself. She could see how Sarah was being ignored and ridiculed, not only by her peers, which was entirely to be expected, but also by her teachers to whom this large-faced child with her intense and often irrelevant observations would talk with either no response, she had noticed, or else rejection. This had happened from the very beginning, she remembered – that first day at school, which she had seen for herself. She had gone along with her sister and their mother to that first day of school, for some reason. None of them in the family had gone to a kindergarten, so this first day of school was Sarah's first time in the world. It had been an acutely embarrassing moment for everyone. Her parents have never spoken about it since – and it was best not to remind them of it, Pamela had added in a quieter voice – because as far as either of them was concerned this moment never happened – and yet the truth of the matter was that Sarah had been unable to interact with the other children in an appropriate way, as teachers call it now. Pamela remembered how unhappy Sarah had been, how reluctant to go to school. As soon as they had got to the school her sister had seemed to freeze. Sarah hadn't wanted to walk through the gates, and so she and her mother had had to make Sarah walk through those gates – one on either side of her, forcing her as it were. There had been a glaze over her sister's eyes, Pamela remembered – not that this was unusual – she had seen it before – it looked as if Sarah had pulled down a cover over her eyes so that she might not be seen. It looked as if she were thinking: I can't see them so they can't see me. When the teacher had called her sister's name, her sister hadn't moved. Go on, Sarah, she remembered their mother saying, although she hadn't actually moved to help her daughter leave them. *Off to the teacher, it's time to go*, their mother had said – *hurry up, you're being a baby.* The teacher kept reading all the other names on her list and all the other children stepped forwards after a hug from their mothers, even tears – all of them, one after the other. When the line of children began to move towards a door, Sarah was still with them, her sister and mother, and not with the children. Surely the teacher has noticed, Pamela said she remembered thinking – surely the teacher or at least one of the other teachers there can see that this child in the uniform isn't joining the others: something has to be done, they can't let the children go in without Sarah – she can't be left behind – but her mother, Pamela was saying in a quieter voice again, seemed to have no intention of actually moving to help her daughter walk towards the children and made no effort other than pushing her daughter's hand off her forearm and stopping her from holding on to her slacks by prising her fingers free, one after the other, and Sarah, who had twisted herself around as if to reach back behind her to the support that kept withdrawing, wasn't looking at the children or her mother but was only staring ahead at a concrete wall. Nobody was doing anything, Pamela was remembering, and it looked as if nobody was ever going to do anything. Sarah's classmates would start school and Sarah would not and all the time she and her mother and Sarah would continue to stand there in the courtyard: the three of them standing, waiting in the courtyard forever.

In the end, the teacher, who had been standing at the door as the children filed in had looked back towards Sarah. She, too, seemed reluctant to come back and get the child who should have been with her. That was how it looked, said Pamela, although she could have been wrong – nobody seemed to want to do anything – it was a farce, she remembered. They might as well all have gone home (and she gone on to her secondary school, she had to assume), but the teacher sent another little girl towards Sarah to invite her to come and the little girl crossed the courtyard with the kind of small smile that shows to the world a pride of purpose, that she, the little girl, had been singled out to do something important, but the moment that the little girl had tried to take Sarah's hand – reaching out roughly, in the way of kids, but no harm intended, anyone could see that – Sarah had pushed her away and then made a rude-looking gesture. She, Pamela, had been mortified to see how her sister had behaved, and became absurdly pleased that the teacher had shouted at her for it (*excuse me!* – so shocked) as she seemed to deserve – and so, at the end of the day – unless it was the end of that first week – she, Pamela, had no time for Sarah's complaints about the *stupid kids*, the *stupid Miss Martin*. It was this little scene, she knew now, which had shaped her annoyance with her sister over the years that came – all the annoyance and impatience, which made it impossible ever to talk to her sister as she might have done otherwise – which made it impossible to have those long sisterly conversations that other people had and which she, not having them, regretted to her great, great sadness. It was only many years later that she ever got to hear what had happened on that day, the first day of school for her sister, at least from Sarah's perspective – the way the other girl had made a grab for Sarah's hand, a grab that had actually hurt her – the nails of the other girl tearing at her skin – that Sarah had been so shocked that the child had done this to her – and then shocked that her gesture of self-defence had been reacted to in such a way – and that all that day and the many days afterwards, she would always be, to the teacher and to the other kids, the one that was *rude* and *defiant* (the teacher's words). Of course, the so-called gesture of self-defence was hardly such a gesture, Pamela told me and the others around us at the wake, I then told my friend Raf as I cleared the table and served the melon cubes he had prepared in a couple of small glass dishes that I once found in a pile on the footpath near the park. The gesture was the finger and couldn't be interpreted as anything else but the finger. Sarah must have learned it from their brother, Pamela had thought at the time and still thought now, and she doubted it could have ever been misinterpreted, even in the mind of a very small child, as only a gesture of self-defence. The finger is the finger, Pamela had told us, there were no two ways about it. Their brother had been an influence, she remembered, he had always been a disturbing and powerful influence, Pamela had then added in that irritating conspiratorial voice she'd kept using throughout the story, and Sarah was far less innocent than any other kid of the very same age – but Sarah had always found it hard to fit in with the subtleties of the social to-ing and fro-ing, all that to-ing and fro-ing that the rest of us acquire early on. From the beginning Sarah had refused to fit in – she had played her own game – and this had annoyed *her* forever, as Pamela put it, but now she could see that it was how her sister had been made – and, in fact, she had heard, through her mother, that their Aunty Anne had been exactly the same – the one who'd left home at fifteen, straight after their brother's funeral, and now lived in Greece, if indeed she still lived in Greece and had not died already or moved somewhere else – nobody knew. I was the only real friend of her sister, she wanted to tell me, Pamela said, and so telling everyone else in the kitchen: I was the only one who didn't leap in and judge her for how she came across. It was such a shame that her sister had to end up at that state school, she then added, as if she were forgetting the fact that I'd gone to that same state school myself, and had never had any chance of going to a different one. It was hardly the best option at the time. Actually it was hardly the only option either. Her going to that state school was the main thing that had undone her sister, Pamela now said. While she still was at SAGS there had always been hope – as soon as her parents had talked about moving Sarah to the state school she (Pamela) had argued against them, as it was the worst possible thing they could have done, given how difficult Sarah had already found being at SAGS, where at least there were decent teachers and decent students and the best will in the world. I, at least, had stuck by her all those years, she said, as if forgetting that I had not gone to SAGS but had gone to the very state school that she was running down, at least by omission – I was the only one to understand her and allow her just to be as she was, which was saying a lot – she said, embarrassing me with the fixity of her look, her apparent attempt to seem sincere to all who were watching, and, as if taking exception to my attempt to resist this look – reacting to my discomfort with her apparent sincerity – she had added: *no, it's true. You have always been a good friend to my sister. Everybody in the family knows this to be true. And it mustn't have been easy*, she now said in a way that made it hard for me to respond. *My sister was never an easy person.* Flicking through the manuscript that Sarah had left on a shelf in her room (and here she showed everyone in the kitchen the manuscript that she must have placed on the bench for the purpose), she had to admit that she'd found it hard to get into what Sarah had written. It puzzled her a lot. It didn't make much sense, she said, but that was Sarah all over. Sarah was like that. She herself was too busy to go through it properly, she said to me then, in front of the others – there was a lot to get through with Sarah's things – she and her brother had a lot of work to do, but she knew I had always been a good friend of Sarah's, she said – and as she knew I had some *literary flair* she was sure she could trust me to see that there was nothing inside it that might embarrass the family. She herself didn't have much experience with things like this and certainly didn't have the time. If I were to have a good look at it first and then type it onto a computer, she or her brother could put it out on one of those self-publishing internet sites in a couple of months, as her husband had suggested; there would be no cost to the family if they did it this way. It was the perfect solution – unless I knew of somewhere else that could be interested, she hinted, some publishing house or an agent, something like that. The family would be grateful if I could help them in this. The title was wonderful, so interesting; the whole thing very interesting, but she could see that the manuscript would need some editing so that it made better sense; the punctuation was confusing at the very least. She had already thought of an image for the front of it – a view from the family beach house. Sarah had always loved the beach house, she knew: sunsets across the water, views looking up from behind the surf club and the houses towards the headland in the winter were the best. They all just thought it might be nice if there were something uplifting left of Sarah in the world *now that she had gone to be with God* – something they could treasure and remember her by.

Of course, at the beginning, I had no intention of reading the manuscript, I had told my friend Raf last night as we forked up the melon pieces, with the wine he had brought seeping into my veins behind the bubbly and pinking up my hands. I took the manuscript with me as I left the wake, with Pamela and her friends and relatives watching me from the door, and that unexpected reference to God – perhaps only a conventional reference, I'd wondered, as it had been proffered, only, at the very last minute, or else, the sort of sign that I should have responded to if I still believed – this reference to God lingering behind me now, in the anxious lines of the hedges and the mondo grass as I crunched along the gravel past the urns, and past the resident from North Ryde Florentine Views, who was sunning himself in his underwear on his own faux Tuscan porch and raising a hand to wave at me without looking up from his belly – not having been able to leave the manuscript, as I'd said, all my attempts to leave it behind having been thwarted by the sister, Pamela. Life is short and art is long, as Flaubert once wrote, I was thinking as I walked to my car, I'd told Raf, carrying the manuscript in its thick plastic Aldi supermarket bag. I have no shortage of books that I know I want to read one day – I have piles by my bed, my bookcases are full. Each time I walk into a second-hand bookshop somewhere I do not emerge from that bookshop without at least three or four purchases; if it is a good-quality bookshop I might emerge with ten. The backs of my diaries contain lists of books I want to read and need to find (the asterisks marking all the *essentials*); every month or so I relent and go on Amazon dot com to trawl their quiet and glowing fields for the *11 used & new available from $3.00.* I have more than enough books that I want to read, more than enough essentials that I spend my time looking for in second-hand bookshops. To discover one new author – and this new author might have been dead for over a hundred years – has always been to discover a new route through the susurrus of those second-hand bookshops, another several evenings trawling the glow of Amazon lists and other better sites. I have no time to think of reading books that I have no interest in reading, I should have told Pamela the first time she brought me the manuscript. Even to take that manuscript home would be an imposition. I already have too many books in my flat, half of which I've not yet read and the manuscript will only add to the weight of those books on my floor. Even without that manuscript I know that more than half of the books in my flat that I've not yet read will be disappointing, I should have told her, I'd told Raf. It is usual that more than half of all the books that I read are complete disappointments. Part of this can be explained by the fact that other people are always giving me books – although not you and I'm thankful for it – either giving them to me as presents or else foisting them on me as partial loans, partial gifts, as books that I should read, which is based on their idea of what I like or at least should like reading, which never at all correlates with the kinds of books that I actually enjoy reading – and while I am usually sure just from reading the first two pages of a book that I will be nothing but disappointed when I read it, I have never allowed myself to give that book away without testing how far this could be true. And yet just to test whether I will be disappointed by a particular book, I always have to overcome my initial distaste for it – I always have to make myself read these books that otherwise I would never look at, never for a moment – I force myself to read these books from beginning to end, I force myself to read them just in case I am wrong. Occasionally I am wrong, although at this moment I cannot recall a single example of this. Often I am impressed, it is true – I am often impressed – I have thought: yes, this book is very well written, it's impressively researched, impeccably edited, it's *a feast of words*, as the blurb has put it, surprisingly correctly; I have often been impressed – overwhelmingly impressed – in this way by the books that I have read and then promptly given away – these books that disappoint me, that fill me with distaste; these books that do nothing but glance off my mind. Yet I force myself to read the books that others give me – these books that weigh the floors of my flat with the impressive descriptions of their contents. I force myself to read them, just in case I am wrong – not so much about the books, I now realise, as I should have told Pamela, but more about my self. I need to force myself to test whether the self I have been protecting and augmenting – this self I have been nourishing on a handful of books and a lifetime of impressions, can withstand the correction of the most impressive of impressive-sounding novels, and yet I am only up to this feat on rare occasions. I need to have energy, or at least a grim determination. I would always much rather reach for one of the books I have already successfully fished from the glow of the internet or the dark of second-hand bookshops on the instinct of someone who fishes by intuition alone; or even better, I should have said to Pamela, I should re-read those books I have already read, which, far from disappointing, have seeped into me through the wounds they have made (this allusion to Kafka here, I remember, having been made chiefly to impress Raf, who, for some reason, I am always trying to impress, I was realising as a sudden crowding of people in numbered sports jackets passed me on the slope by the bins near Marcel's).

I am a difficult-to-please reader. Most of what I read disappoints before too long. I must have a peculiar taste in literature, I should have said to Pamela; most of what others like to read does nothing but disappoint and then accrete into a pullulating pile of distaste, I had told Raf, I was remembering as I wondered about stepping among the people in the crowd – this need to weave among them, to make my way against the tide of people coming into the city and up the ramp from Central Station, so that I might not crash my body into any of them, this weaving taking all of my concentration for a moment, and being soothing somehow, entirely right. My father might be a writer – or at least call himself a writer, and has always called himself a writer – desperate to write, as he has always said, the one book, the one brilliant book he knows he will write, and of which he has written drafts and drafts, none of them quite *getting there* since everything and everyone around him has always conspired to make it impossible for him to get there; his time is coming to a desperate end – he has cancer – and so what he has done is only what he has done and what he keeps trying to do every day of his life, and in that sense he is still a writer even though he has not published anything more than that book *Fame and the Infamous: Noteworthy Inhabitants of Ku-ring-gai Shire* that I know of – this book that he would pull from the shelves of his friends and tear into bits so he could paper his naked self before streaking down their driveways and up the winding streets of the gully just to stop them reading it or at least to stop them taking it seriously – if only he had the chance, he's often said, and the guts, and I – although neither Raf nor Pamela could know (if I could have dared to tell them), I was thinking – I live for months and months on a few phrases alone: trying again and again and again to write even as I continue to fail, to fail to be the writer that I promised to be at high school, my father all over again, although in fact much poorer, since while he writes thousands of pages of words, I have, until Saturday, written almost nothing at all. I am the very last person Pamela should ever have asked to look at what Sarah had written during her last years alive, I would have liked to be able to tell my friend Raf. However, I did tell him that I am immune to the pathos of circumstances. The fact that Sarah had lived (very much alone) as Pamela had described that day she rang me about the death, and then died (as she had also described), still had not made me curious to read the manuscript and had certainly not made me sympathetic to reading it in the way that this information might have made others sympathetic or at least curious about what it could contain. I could never be a reviewer, I'd said – not a genuine reviewer nor professional reader. I am completely out of touch with what makes others curious or sympathetic to the idea of reading a manuscript that has been written by someone who lived and then died as her sister Pamela described. Every time I pass a bookshop that has the latest releases and the latest promotions of fiction in the window, I am never curious about anything that lies inside the pages whose thick white tongues have been spread just a little so that it is plain for all to see that the type has been spaced too much and the book made thicker and heavier than it might have been, and certainly more than what the book – as it appears to me – has necessarily warranted. All the new novels that are published these days are thicker and heavier than the novels themselves would usually warrant. Each of them is thicker and heavier, by virtue of the fact that the pages are thicker than they should have been and the type spaced further apart than it should have been and the cover made thicker than it should have been in the mistaken belief that the worth of a novel is always only equivalent to its thickness and weight and that the more of it you have when you buy it, the more likely you have bought something worthwhile or at least worth the excessive thickness and heaviness that the publisher has made of it. In reality, I was thinking as I stood there, becoming conscious that there was a bookshop around the corner and that I needed to make sure that, today at least, I didn't enter it – in reality the writer would have had no intention for her or his manuscript (of a novel) to be made so thick and heavy that it took away room from everything else in the house of the person who had bought it. While the writer might have often laughed at the excessive size of her or his friends' editions of *War and Peace* or *In Search of Lost Time* – making fun, as others did, of the width of the volumes and the implied verbosity this suggests – in reality, too, the writer might never once have questioned the decision by a few marketing experts to thicken and add weight to their own modest tale so that it not only turned into something that was taller than the only volume of *In Search of Lost Time* that the writer had ever partially read, but it became heavier, too. This manuscript of Sarah's, I might have said to Pamela, as I told Raf, could very easily become one of these over-sized novels in the windows of bookshops. The title of the manuscript was alluring, and if that was a prime consideration – taken together with the pathos of the circumstances of its discovery in a dead woman's room – it was likely that it could become one of those over-sized novels that are slightly fanned open in the windows of bookshops. But if this were so I would be the last person to give an opinion on the merits of what Sarah had written in the manuscript. The over-sized novels in windows are usually the first ones that I give away as soon as I can; I give them away once I read them because they invariably disappoint. If they had been produced as slimmer volumes – in a shape more fitting to the content – it might have been possible, I've always thought, that I could have kept one or two and given them a second attempt at a reading, but as it was the very size and weight of these novels have prejudiced me – and particularly my sense of having been tricked when I find myself turning the pages of the novels too quickly, with the overwhelming disgust of someone who cannot stop munching through boxes and boxes of vacuous snacks. I am easily put off, I should have said to Pamela, but instead said to Raf. My reactions are completely topsy-turvy to everyone else in the world, or at least everyone else that I have known – intelligent people all of them: the very readers publishers dream of – who, far from nurturing disgust, find nothing more delicious and satisfying than holding a newly bought, tall, heavy novel – a recent release – whose long nights of reading they look forward to with pleasure because the very thingness of the novel has been infused with a certain satisfaction by the years and months of reading similarly tall, heavy novels while propped up, sitting in bed. The books that are necessary to me are only boring to others, I have long come to realise, and as I needed to have said to Sarah's sister, Pamela. I am a freak, I should have said to her: my opinion worth nothing, my thoughts about the manuscript she had given me, *Panthers and the Museum of Fire*, therefore of no value to anyone at all.

Quite apart from this prejudice, I had then thought of going on to say to Raf, but hadn't – a prejudice about which he had heard me rant on a number of occasions – there was another problem, and this was the fact that the title of the manuscript was rich and suggestive – so rich and suggestive that, even though the title was nothing but the wording of a road sign that anybody living in Sydney could recognise, the lure of it was apparent to me the moment I saw it. If I had been reluctant to read the manuscript as soon as I heard about its existence, I now knew that I would never want to read this manuscript simply because the title was rich and suggestive. Even if I had not had a prejudice against over-sized novels that sit in the windows of bookshops with their pages slightly fanned, I would always have been envious of the title; I was envious of the triumph of that coup. Yes, I was envious of the title, I might have admitted to Raf, as this was the kind of irritable admission that it was usually okay to display to this particular very old friend and especially at one of our extended, shapeless dinners. I had to face this fact: I was too envious of the title, and what it suggested about the contents of the manuscript, as I'd thought of it then, to ever have had the guts to read it without a gun being placed at my temple first. Sarah might have died – she might have died friendless, apparently unmissed, but she had left behind her, as it is said, this manuscript about a road sign – a manuscript with the coup of having the wording of a sign as its title – a manuscript which might even become a novel that is sold and sells well on the strength of the title alone. All my life, I would like to have been able to tell my friend Raf, with a gesture of extravagance (as I imagined it now, on the slope below the bus station), I have been envious of people I have known who have managed to write novels, even though I have not had the inspired perseverance to write one myself. I have been envious of this person and that person who have written novels; just to know that I once knew them has been enough to make me envious of that person who has written novels, whereas of a completely unknown person who has written novels, I have found that I have no envy of either them or their novels at all. I have always thought of myself as a writer of novels in the making, I was thinking, even though I have published very little – almost nothing at all – and have in fact come to a grinding halt – as you know very well (I would have liked to be able to say to Raf). I have always wanted to write novels – more than anything else in this life I have wanted to write novels that I could hold in my hand – and yet I haven't had the perseverance to get anywhere near this achievement; all the words that I intend to write evaporate as soon as I think of them, and when I look back on my life, all I see are these words I have intended to write: all the thousands and millions of words I would like to have put down on paper (or if not on paper, onto the luminous, uncaring face of a screen). I have hoped to write thousands and millions of words, words that plume into the air around the person who is my self as I would like to seem to others, but all these imagined words, while they thicken the air about me can only mean nothing to me, just as they mean, of course, nothing to others, except to keep up the pretence (to my self) that I am still a writer of novels in the making; all my attempts, my failures at writing novels have come to nothing more than this: the delusion that, despite the evidence of my absolute failure (and the related evidence of my father, my flesh and blood, who manages still to spill his words into the gully he lives in, filling it to the brim with words that will never be read), I am still a writer of novels in the making and that one day I will hold a novel in my hands and that this novel I am holding will be mine. I don't like to think of myself as an envious person, I would have then liked to say to my friend Raf with another gesture of extravagance, but thinking now about my first reactions to the manuscript – thinking as clearly as I can about my reactions at the wake when Pamela had mentioned the existence of the manuscript, the manuscript she thought I should look at – I can feel the chill in my chest as if I were feeling it a second time: the chill of my never-sleeping envy.

I was realising that, out of everything I had heard that day at the funeral, there was nothing that set me against my one-time friend more than this manuscript of a novel that Pamela had wanted me to look at. All the years that I had known her Sarah had never once talked about wanting to write novels, I was thinking now that I had made myself put my phone in my bag and walk around the corner away from Marcel's, past the shop of remaindered books and other treasures that I must resist now – and especially now, I was thinking, since my way forwards as a writer has become so clear following this breakthrough on Saturday as I have been calling it – a breakthrough, which, I suspect, I will never be able to discuss with Raf. How was it then that Sarah had written this manuscript that might or might not have the potential to become a novel in a bookshop? I had spent years – decades even – in my own hopeless wrangling with words in my head that had come to nothing, and all Sarah had done was to hide herself in a hole of a place, no better and perhaps even worse than mine, so that she could write (and finish, very obviously) a manuscript called *Panthers and the Museum of Fire* and then, in a final, brilliant moment of inspiration, die in her romantic – even if not at all romantic – way. This late flowering of her writing (of a possible novel in a bookshop) had taken the form in my thoughts, during the days that followed the funeral, of Sarah, as I remember her, laughing at the hopelessness of my own attempts – all the attempts which, since her death, could no longer be hidden – this way that we assume that nothing is hidden after someone has died, I was thinking as I walked on; I'd seen her laughing, in my head: the coup of her turning an apparently wasted life around, as they say; giving it form in her writing; she was making a mockery of all the hours and years that I had spent doing the same, or at least an attempt of the same, but to no issue at all. She had spent a year or two writing this manuscript of a novel, if I am to believe Pamela (although on what basis, I don't know), but I had spent decades – nearly all of my life in failing to write even a repetition of my one-time *far-fetched* magazine despite my bargaining with God near the end of school that shrivels me as I think of it again. In itself, the manuscript about the road sign – this potential novel, which I was, at first, refusing to read – had made of me a bitter and envious enemy, and this I *would* have said had I been able to articulate my poisonous thoughts to Raf. There was no way that I was going to read this manuscript, this possible novel, I should have said to Pamela and, later, to Raf. I already hated it more than anything else in the world.

But, of course, as I had gone on to say to Raf while I emptied an own-brand packet of almond thins on a plate between us, skipping all these thoughts about the manuscript, the poisonous parts of my thoughts after my reference to *Fame and the Infamous: Noteworthy Inhabitants of Ku-ring-gai Shire* – my performance becoming truly magnificent, as I hoped, with this disclosure: Pamela's phone call on Friday changed all that. She had wanted me to return the manuscript – and to return it unread *if I didn't mind* – and that was enough to prompt me to do the very opposite of what she had asked me to do. Pamela had rung me two days after the funeral, to check that I hadn't started on it yet and to plan to meet, *to catch up over a coffee*, as she put it in the most unctuous of syllables – although really to get the thing back from me for her own reasons (no reasons were given) – and she would have had no idea that it was her very request to return the manuscript unread as soon as I could that had been the only thing to prompt me to get round to reading the pages that she had insisted I read but hadn't yet read and had never had any intention of reading. She rang me on the mobile and so she had probably congratulated herself that she had done her all to prevent me from reading the manuscript; she would have imagined me heading back to sleep after the call, glad to put my head on the pillow after being rung so late. She would have imagined that she had saved the situation by ringing me so soon, so soon after the funeral and before the weekend, and that our arrangement for the Monday morning *first thing*, as she said, although still three days away, would guarantee its being saved from my curious eyes; don't worry, I've saved the day, I could hear her telling her parents or herself – whoever she had promised to get the manuscript back for: lucky I got her mobile number at the wake. Jenny won't have started it. She wouldn't have had the time.

I had been quiet for some minutes after I announced to Raf that I had agreed to hand the manuscript back, supposedly unread as requested. My entire performance to him yesterday evening had built up to the announcement of this grandiloquent act of deception I was planning, a rhetorical flourish for the benefit of my friend. This is how it has always been with Raf, I now real-ised as I entered the mouth of the tunnel under the railway lines, still walking against the main flow of the pedestrians who were emerging from the tunnel Into the daylight, while I moved from the sun to the fluorescent lights. Raf and I, we bring to our dinners together a collection of anecdotes that one of us presents to the other as a pretext for a string of jokes, or, even better, a rant – one of those long and luxurious exaggerations that each of us enjoys more than anything else. All the time when we are away from each other, each of us husbands a likely anecdote, and this we keep alive and warm until the next time we see each other, I was thinking as I walked by a thick group of what might have been tourists who were looking at some intricate cut paper greeting cards set out on a wrinkled towel at the lip of the wall tiles – at least that is what I do, and if Raf does the same, I can only wonder whether he keeps his anecdotes from any of his other friends – the friends that he usually tells me about in such detail that even the stories they tell him about other people stay in my mind – or if, when he tells them the anecdotes that he has been saving for me, he has already grown sick of the sound of them or maybe, with the retelling, they are only savoured the more.

But when Raf had asked me to assess the manuscript as a manu-script yesterday, to say whether it was any good at all or just a piece of junk, as he had said, leaning back against my kitchen wall, his eyes half-closed, his eyebrows raised as if he were ready to assess it there in front of him, inviting me to hand it over (which I didn't) – I had been taken more than a little off guard, as I intended to tell him the next time I saw him, now that I had given more mind to the problem, or so I told myself as I went deeper into the tunnel – confronting him with the truth about ourselves, as I saw it. I hadn't expected the question and so really I hadn't got to say what I wanted to say. Although I had said that the manuscript was everything that I had expected it to be, and made much of the ridiculous idea of the holiday house cover that Pamela was planning – with a sunset as she had suggested – the streaks of pink, gold and very pale turquoise and ultramarine that every dubious religion, every cult, every whacko organisation spreads in gloss over its pamphlets – going on and on about the sunset colours and the holiday house on the front – although I had said all this, I also knew all along that the manuscript as a manuscript had actu-ally affected me, and the reason for this has probably a lot to do with my own weakness, my own susceptibility, my own essentially gullible nature, because of course the manuscript was nothing and yet I liked it because I am a fool.

In all the years that we have known each other, I decided I should tell Raf, as I have often meant to tell him but repeatedly failed to do so, we have been anxious not to reveal ourselves to be fools. We have clowned with each other – each of us trying to outdo the other in our attempts to describe ourselves in the most ridiculous and therefore the most flattering, careful light possible – but this wasn't the same thing as revealing ourselves to be fools. We have told stories about ourselves in which we have failed to recog-nise somebody, failed to complete something or *have gone over the top*, as we put it in our conversations with each other: gone over the top in trying to impress somebody important, only to discover they are not that important person we were thinking them to be but just the boyfriend of the publicist who had managed to get a ticket and who enjoyed coming to such occasions for free drinks as much as we did ourselves. We have told stories in which we are abject and subservient, in which our colleagues rate us poorly, in which we make fun of those same colleagues or our friends or our family and then those same colleagues or friends or family members find out about what we have said in circumstances that are either highly embarrassing or shameful. Where we cheapskate for wedding presents but regret it too late to do anything about it; where the conversation dies away leaving our last superficial comment naked and loud; where we have mistaken our old schoolfriends for their mothers and then compounded the embarrassment by apologising; where we make jokes as we join a gathering only to find the gathering going quiet all of a sudden; where we are convinced that our mouths belong to somebody else, our words in somebody else's gullet – somebody who hates us; where late at night we imagine the unfolding scenes of our own humiliation to the soundtrack of a recent, maudlin, overrated film; where we emerge shamefaced and mildly drunk from an event to which we were never even invited, only to remember that everything we have said was actually said aloud, not just in our heads; where we come to the relieved conclusion that nobody we know can read our minds, so long as we can keep the words from escaping; where our worst interpretation of what somebody has just said is always the one that is proved correct by the events that follow it, one after the other, now out of our control and even exceeding what we once described to each other as *our very worst nightmare*. All this we have told each other over the years that we have known each other, each of our anecdotes very likely having an origin in fact. We have clowned for each other – playing the fool – but this is not at all the same as revealing ourselves to be fools; we have played the fool to each other but this is completely different from revealing ourselves to be the fool behind the fool that is playing. The fool behind the fool is the one who no longer plays, I was thinking as I tried to catch what I could of the conversations of the people who surrounded me in the tunnel – not so much of what the other people were saying, which was impossible given the echoes of footsteps that distorted the words, but the music of their talking, which I suddenly realised I hadn't heard for a while. The fool behind the fool is the one who either cannot play or forgets to play and so keeps hold of their moment too long: who stands with the present for the wedding or the lips puckered for a kiss – and shows she had wanted that kiss or that giving of the present in full view; who lets the tears course down her cheeks as the music crescendos at the climax of a film. Who reads the manuscript of a one-time friend and at the end of it cannot say whether the piece is good or bad; for whom words are not yet ready, only images and phrases (and not even these), but who finds that she has been changed by the reading – come to a breakthrough by the reading – and yet in all honesty, as she would have to describe it, is unable to say to her supposedly good friend Raf why or how that is.

For years I have wanted to say something like this to Raf, I realised as I kept walking through the tunnel under the station and trying to catch the essence of other people talking, against the louder thrums and notes of the buskers, as well as the walking, my mind at least beginning to grow calm as I listened for the words; buoyed by the music of conversation in a tunnel as it were – its very ordinariness the source of its pleasure – the intonation which I could follow, could hum: an *interesting diversion*, as I might have called it if I wanted to make light of the experience to my friend.

Of course, as I now told myself while pausing near a man who was setting up a stool near the wall, a large, black case stickered over with worn paper squares in front of him – a case of a very unlikely shape, I was thinking, for an instrument: I have already told my friend Raf about the manuscript and the funeral, offering my tale of it as a story. Too late to go back to it now. Whenever Raf and I get together, we are always exchanging stories of this kind: one of us telling the tale and the other of us laughing. This is what I like best about my old friend Raf. In fact, I have always thought of Raf as my first real friend, I was thinking as I moved off again, becoming aware as I walked that my heels were starting to get sore. Although I have had many friends in my life, until the point when I met him, Raf was the first person I ever decided to be friends with – all my life until that point I had been surrounded by friends, but these friends were only friends so long as we saw each other in the ordinary course of our lives, I had begun to realise during my early years at university. The friends I made in the first primary school I went to, for example, became ex-friends the moment that I moved schools – then, since nobody from that primary school went to the same high school, the friends I had made in the second primary school were lost – and this was the same, I had realised, for the friends made outside of school: the friends I made at ballet and the friends I made at softball. When it was winter, I never used to think of my softball friends – I said goodbye to them at the last match or the prize-giving day and didn't think of them again until the next season started – even when it was summer and I saw them twice a week – once at the training and the second time at the game – it never occurred to me to think of them between those times; I certainly didn't ring them. And this was the same for my ballet friends. When I wasn't doing pliés, the friends I made at ballet might well have not existed, except in the way the building in which I did my pliés existed, as did the teacher and the barre and the mirrors – I certainly didn't ring them; I never thought of their houses, I never thought of their phones – it was very likely that my parents had had the numbers of my ballet and softball friends, I was now thinking as I walked through the tunnel – at least the softball friends. My parents shared the driving with the parents of some of the other girls doing the sport, but if they had the numbers, I never thought about those numbers – it would never have occurred to me to ask for those friends' numbers so that I could ring them on the weekend or in the evening or during the long and shapeless holidays that I would welcome as I would also welcome sleep; it never occurred to me to think of ringing them so that I might see them at any other time; while I was perfectly happy seeing my friends and talking to them during their allotted time in my life, I remember realising some time ago, when I was still at university, I was also perfectly happy not seeing them or talking to them when they were not there. If any of them saw me or talked to me at another time, it was entirely due to their own efforts: the efforts of their parents, when we were at primary school, and of themselves later at high school. I never made the effort myself – indeed, I would not have known how to make the effort, I had only realised, when I heard of a softball friend who visited another in hospital after that accident with a ball that crushed the side of her skull – sadly, perhaps, I wouldn't have known what to do – I was also happy enough, however, about not knowing how to make the effort. I used to think that if I were to make the effort to ring someone and actually to invite them over for a chat or out for a film, something would be created that I wouldn't have known how to control; something would be created, which, having energy in itself, its own inner momentum, would hook into my skin and kill me if it could – I would be creating something dangerous, I must have realised – and just to control this dangerous thing I would eventually have to kill it before it killed me – and yet I would never be able to kill any living thing, I had always thought – not a mouse nor a cockroach nor a moth nor an ant – I would never be able to kill any living thing with a cold intent. I would never be able to live with it. I would rather not initiate any contact outside of the day-to-day hours when I usually saw that person, because by initi-ating it I would have to take responsibility for that contact, as I can imagine people describing it in books somewhere now, and already, without putting it into words myself at the time – without trying to think it through as I was now trying to think it through while I walked – I know I'd avoided this responsibility with a fierce timidity. And it was even the same with my friendship with Sarah, I was thinking both then and now: she always rang me, I never rang her – but at university, I was realising as I walked close to the turgid shine of the wall tiles in the tunnel, I had obviously begun to think differently. At university I had become impressed by the way that the others around me – my friends (my acquaintances, actually, I now corrected myself) – seemed able to conduct very brief conversations with other people as, walking along, they might chance to meet when they moved between buildings. It was the nature of these conversations that had impressed me, I know: the way the simplest exchange of 'how are you?' or 'what's been happening?' would engender the lightest, most effortless, but very elegant small exchange of words; the way something other, quite beautiful and detailed would arise with a few choice phrases, and phrases which had their own momentum, their own limitations, their own inbuilt intuition for rhythm and decay. For the first time it occurred to me to want to learn how to make these same kinds of conversations – for no other reason, I was remembering now as I moved further into the thick of the commuters in the tunnel – for no other reason than for the most aesthetic of reasons – the same reasons that might lead somebody else to learn how to dance the tango in the way the tango needed to be danced. I wanted to be able to conduct these same kinds of conversations – these very lightest and most elegant of conversations – and so, without pausing to worry about my ability to control them, I began to use these same phrases – these 'how are yous?' and 'what's been happenings?' – and actually became skilled at fashioning the fiction of my replies. Nobody, I must have worked out for myself from pure observation, referred to any pain or difficulty except through the lightest of references; any pain or difficulty seemed always to be transformed into an entertaining lilt of sentences – a single lilt of words with the simplest of grammar – and the more expert the speaker, the more effortless the sentence, with the most expert decorating their difficulties by adding a short and single subordinated clause. A three-day headache, for example, would become the prelude for at last being up to a full week of partying again; the funeral of an aunt would be inserted into a list of comic woes, and for no other reason than to get a laugh and a cheerful reply. All pains or difficulties had to have that function, I must have realised, thinking of it now, and so each one needed to be managed in the most skilful way possible, so that it became the incongruous component, the one that got the laugh. I became expert in this dallying of my difficulties: I even invented them, or embellished – everything was embellishment – in a lilting series of sentences, each one delivered or performed like a dance, and my reward, as it seemed, was not only the satisfaction of the dance but also the earning of imagined accolades: of the 'she's great', 'she's so laid back', 'she makes me laugh', or so I was remembering as I heard, from far back in the tunnel behind me, the man with the unknown instrument in the stickered-over case (a kind of lyre, I thought as I recalled what I had seen in his hands, or a flat kind of harp) beginning to play something that could have been jazz, unless it were another busker playing, someone I had failed to notice.

And yet in thinking about this dance of sentences, I have concertinaed many months. I have concertinaed many processes, too, because I actually don't remember connecting what I was doing with the sentences and the earning of the titles of 'great' and 'laid back', which I evidently craved. It is always afterwards that such connections become obvious, and in thinking them through (even writing them down on screens such as this one), such connections seem so inevitable as to suggest that they had been obvious at the time. I have always concertinaed events and concocted connections; I am always being duped into thinking that there is, somewhere, a clear connection between all events and outcomes in my life. But in reality nothing was obvious then and is not obvious now (and is still not obvious, as I can see now, four years later). I make connections between one event or series of events and an apparent outcome in my head and this connection, seemingly obvious, has always been false. All my life I have witnessed my brain working in this way, I was thinking as I got closer and closer to the hub of the station near the end of the tunnel. Even now: I had clearly decided to walk to the café, setting off much earlier than I might have needed to set off for that particular café, so that I might have time to turn over all the thoughts in my head before seeing the sister again and handing over the manuscript; all my life – or at least since the time that I was anorexic, when to walk was the ultimate pleasure, the only existence possible – I have attempted to understand my self by taking walks and I have always arrived somewhere with apparently more simply formulated thoughts and a sense that thinking is possible, and that I know what I'm doing or at least what I have been trying to do. I make connections as I walk, I was realising as I got closer and closer to the end of the tunnel, and I am always being buoyed by the unexpected, serendipitous connections between one train of thought and another, and yet the connections that I fashion in my brain through the repetitive, inevitable rhythm of my walking could well have no reality, no veracity, I was realising, or trying to realise, outside these peculiar ambulatory conditions of my mind – as for example here, I told myself now that I had decided to turn into the newsagency at the station. I compress all events and apparent outcomes in my thinking, I was noticing as I entered the crush near the entrance of the shop, by the newspaper piles and lottery balloons, in the way that my bones and my ligaments are compressed as I walk. It is a thoroughly artificial way of thinking, I couldn't help observing as I moved further and further into the newsagency, towards the section with the notebooks near the back of it – a way of thinking that relies on the compression of ligaments and bones. I should force myself to think outside the inevitable compression of thoughts; I have to fight to resist the compulsion to compress my ideas. I have to work against the effects of walking even if I have to keep on walking, to clear the space in my mind that will soon, invariably, be fast crowded in on by the compression of every thought that occurs when I walk.

It was only then, in the newsagency at the end of the tunnel, where I had to stop walking, since, as it happened, I had got to the very back of the shop, that I had any chance of being able to force myself beyond what seemed otherwise to be turning into a satisfying conclusion in my thinking. I made myself look at the epithets of 'great' and 'laid back', forcing myself to see that there was no necessary connection between these epithets and my developing a fictional lilt of small talk in my later university days. I had indeed developed this small talk for no other reason than aesthetic pleasure, and yet I'd had no aim, nor desire for the epithets, I was thinking then in the newsagency under the railway lines. I have no actual recall of wanting the epithets for myself. By drawing a connection between the epithets and the small talk I have made an unpardonable stoop to the cliché – and one that Raf would only laugh at, I was realising as I loitered by the notebooks, tempted as I am always being tempted by the pregnant possibilities of their compact weight and sweet-smelling unmarked pages. I have to force my brain to resist such automatic and baseless compressions – I have to force it to think away from the always tempting and seemingly inevitable acts of baseless compressions and conclusions – and I have begun to think in this way, I was telling myself, because I am trying to uncover, without resorting to walking, something prior to my decision to call Raf my first, real friend. I have begun this train of thought after realising that, even to begin to call Raf my first, real friend, there must have been a time when to have friends had meant something entirely different from the kind of friendship I began with Raf, and that friendship with Raf, at the beginning, was not only qualitatively different from all prior friendships but also so removed from the category of these friendships that I might have decided – as I did, I remember – to call my friendship with Raf a first, real friendship, as a way of distinguishing it from every other friendship I had made in my life until that point.

I remember initiating what I called to myself a friendship with Raf as a departure from what I usually did when it came to the category of friends. This is what I remember: this departure, this taking a course that had never been taken before. And yet I don't remember that I took this course with any sense of the risk of departing from my usual behaviour with the category of friends. Since it had been unusual for me to act in this way – and not only unusual, but completely uncharacteristic – there should have been some awareness of the risk of my behaviour, and yet I have no memory of risk; no sense that what I was about to do would release the uncontrollable monster of others in my life. Perhaps it was because I was still anorexic, I was thinking as I tried to think of this time. When I was an anorectic I was fearless: there was no moment of recoil or decision to talk myself out of irrational reactions, in the way that we are always being led to believe that people who have irrational fears, say, of insects or water, do their best, once they decide to act, to talk themselves out of their irrational fear and into an acceptance of the more ordinary and usually unsurprising characteristics of the insects or water that they have feared for most of their lives. In fact, it was only afterwards, in the long undifferentiated state of being that could be called post-anorexic adulthood, that I even came to read the kinds of articles about people who have irrational fears and about what it is best to do when you are in that situation. At the time – although technically an adult already – I was innocent of these stories of overcoming odds, both physical and emotional, which still seem to be published these days in every magazine in the country, I was thinking as I looked about me in the newsagency, and in every other newspaper, as an alternative to the tragic news story or gossip about the famous. Although an adult and therefore prey to the constant fodder of newspapers and magazines, as well as having my first unlimited access to the seamless imbecility of television, I had quite failed to immerse myself sufficiently in its narrative soup: where stories about overcoming odds are only included in a careful calculation to not lose the readership that would otherwise be so irritated by the lives of the famous or depressed by the tragedy of news stories that they would refuse to buy another magazine or weekend newspaper ever again in their lives. In fact, I was only realising as I looked back at the selection of notebooks in preference to the magazines whose disorganised physical presence – particularly the ugly juxtaposition of headlines and shining skin on the covers – has only ever depressed me, it's not only in weekend newspapers and magazines, and on radio of course, that this kind of good news story – this help-yourself story, as couched in articles whose slow-developing anxiety is calculated to make you begin to search your own skin for symptoms as you read – is, in fact, the same kind of story that is often served up on television, and not only on the news magazine programs, I was thinking: it isn't only there. Most of the movies I have seen on television recently or on the net, as well as quite a few that I have seen in the cinema, are based on this same dubious formula of the good news story – the very basic aspects of this story, admittedly – but nothing short of the formula that there have to be odds overcome and a normalising life achieved by the end of the film, and that the story, no matter how specific or unusual, has to fit into something larger than itself, which could only be this supposed normalising life; so that this larger, very nebulous but normalising life won't be undermined by the questionings, the irrationalities or the accidents but actually come to be strengthened by all the deviations from it, by the beautiful and uplifting and always recognisable coming-to-resolution moments at the end of the film, in the way that the good news story always finishes with the reminder of the tiny, even imperceptible, ways that the irrational or unfortunate still are able to blend the peculiarities of their misfortunes into the greater web of an over-familiar and sentimentalised normalising life that is presumed to surround us, so that the *feel of a triumphant act of normalising* is unshakeable, even inescapable, at the end.

Perhaps it was because I was still so young, I started to understand as I took up one notebook in my hand and then put it back to take up another – all the time conscious that a woman with sleek, brown hair was standing next to me and probably trying to decide between the same set of notebooks – perhaps it was because I was still so young back then that there was no sense of taking a departure from my usual behaviour when I decided to initiate a friendship with Raf. When you are young, I told myself at the back of the newsagency as I stood next to the (most likely) much younger woman who seemed to be doing the same thing that I was – trying to decide whether to buy a notebook, even though I knew I already had an oversupply of notebooks that I never use, as if the buying of one more, perhaps more fitting, notebook would

turn out to be the best thing I have ever done on behalf of the self
that still longs to write in the way that I longed to write without
issue before the time of my breakthrough – when you are young,
I was thinking, you are still attempting to form an idea of what an
unnormalised life might be. You have been in rebellion from the
normalising life that has been forced on you by your parents and
have made various but often incomplete and utterly unsuccessful
attempts to be in rebellion from the normalising life of your peers.
It is inevitable that the young person becomes convinced that they
are the first to see clearly what others have failed to see; that they
judge eighty to ninety per cent of the population to be bogged in
imbecility and that they alone (with very few intellectual compa-
triots) are the only ones to have the daring and the capacity to
resist. And yet, this daring of the young is nothing more than
the energy of their youth and their apparent clarity of seeing only
the measure of their innocence, I told myself as I replaced the
last notebook I had taken to inspect, being determined now to
resist the urge to buy a new one that always overcomes me in the
meanest of newsagencies. All the energy expelled by the young in
the éclat of their revelation forms the glow that surrounds them,
moves with them as they move, and is the one cause of all envious
thoughts by those who are no longer young – for the first time
ever, thinking of myself in the second category and no longer the
first. It is the glow given off by young bodies and the young minds
in those bodies; this is what older people envy, I was thinking as
I continued to stand at the back of the newsagency, staring at the
notebooks, and becoming very aware that the younger woman had
moved on, and was probably already out in the open air or inside
a train – even if there is no cause to envy what is only the innocent
energy of that young person's ignorance and gullibility. We realise
it is only this innocent energy that forms the glow on the skin and
the grace in all the gestures of the young and yet we envy them this
glow, this excretion of their youth. Every day we are newly struck
by the ignorance and gullibility at the source; we never cease to
be irritated by the unromantic physiological origins of the glow,

and yet we continue to live in bitter and base envy of the young; we are no better than our parents were, I was thinking as I forced myself to turn around and walk back towards the entrance of the newsagency, nor any of the most short-tempered, unimaginative denigrators of the young. We never seem to learn from our own experience, let alone from the many tiers of generations that have piled themselves into the centuries before us.

It was with all these thoughts turning around in my mind that I bent down next to the wall outside the newsagency to reach into my bag for my phone again, so that I might check the time. I have been thinking about Raf – about my friendship with Raf – and yet really, I thought as I reached around among the odd bits of things I keep in my bag, I have only been thinking about my self. It's always this way: I attempt to push my thoughts outwards, away from my person, and yet I always end up thinking exclusively about my self. My friendship with Raf has been an exception, I know: not only in the past but also very recently as well. I have this friendship with Raf and it is probably the only friendship that has continued from my youth these past twenty years: it's as if there could only be one real friendship that I could allow in my existence, and that my deciding to initiate a friendship with Raf was to take that one chance of friendship and thereby lock all others out; I had decided to initiate a friendship with Raf, and this had comprised the simple invitation of whether he felt like having a coffee with me at the Student Union after one of our third-year Archaeology tutorials – I had extended the invitation for coffee in the same way I had been conducting my lilting greetings conversations – I remember asking the very question about the coffee with the same intonation as 'how are you?'; I had taken pleasure in pronouncing this invitation in much the same way I had taken pleasure in conducting the lightest of light and graceful greetings even though, all the time, I know I was aware that me asking Raf to coffee might have been seen as an attempt at a come-on – an attempt which I would never have dared to make, and especially back then – Raf having been, the whole time I have known him, immune from come-ons from people like me – all the relationships that he has had over the years having always occurred in a place and among a group of people that has never included me – a fact – at least a supposed fact – that must have been the one thing that convinced me that this friendship was a prospect at all. It was more an accumulation of purely aesthetic, technical pleasure, I told myself, that had set this friendship in motion – and as such it must have been one of the rare moments in my life that this act could possibly have occurred. Ever since initiating my friendship with Raf, I have found that the same anxiety about other people has returned: I have allowed myself to protect the notion of making time for my friendship with Raf but all other friendships have become so much more than I can cope with, as it seems – I am always becoming anxious about being able to cope with seeing anything at all of other people, but my friendship with Raf is completely immune. It is as if my old friend Raf has been absorbed into my own existence, become indistinguishable from my existence, and all other people need to be kept at a distance by my more or less successful attempts at a lilting banter. And yet, since my university days, I have lost the energy for this banter, I was thinking as I tucked my phone into my jacket pocket having checked that there was a little time yet before I had to be there at the café: I know it is possible still to engage in it, but, like a one-medal athlete, I know I am past my prime. I have lost what I thought was my unshakeable capacity for the exuberant energy of the lilting nothings of the sorts of conversations I once so deftly emulated and pursued – and perhaps still manage to emulate in my meetings up with Raf – and so find myself either overloading my conversations with extraneous and intense verbal matter – as with my colleagues at the radio station, and my recent connection with that woman from downstairs in the block of flats whenever we happen to link up on our walks around Black Wattle Bay – this woman, called either Laura or Lucy – I can never remember – who always listens to what I say and, I fear, becomes quickly over-whelmed and easily tired – or, seeing that a conversation needs to be made with someone, and is expected to be made, I move away and try to make sure I haven't been seen. It is as if I am a cannibal, I was reflecting as I began to head away from the newsagency towards the stairs that would get me up to ground level again – I am a cannibal because I have absorbed Raf into the uncertain and always jittery and mostly completely defended territory of my self. I have absorbed my friend Raf and so to think about him as separate from myself is likely to be impossible. All the time between the first phone call from Pamela – from then to the funeral and to the reading of the manuscript – I know I'd been aware that I had been looking forward to seeing my friend Raf as soon as I could, but even as I thought of him and was savouring what seemed to be the delicious thread that is the anticipation I always feel when I know I am going to be seeing him and *telling him something*, I have never made an effort to digest what surely must be indigestible: that this, my friendship with Raf, is my one, my only exception to what has to be my base incapacity to cope with friendships with other people and to whom all my associations with other people have always been surrendered in the pleasure of telling a tale to get a laugh – that nothing and no one has been spared from this pleasure of mine, and especially not my old friend Sarah, the one who is dead.

And yet I had been making myself think of Sarah and her manuscript when I had walked to the shops before Raf arrived yesterday, I was remembering as I got closer both to the escalators and to the stairs that led to the daylight on the other side of the tunnel under the railway lines. I had been thinking all yesterday and the day before of her manuscript, and the breakthrough I had come to in my own writing – I had rung my friend because I was wound, so tightly wound from reading and writing and the excitement of my breakthrough, because I needed to go out and get moving – and it was only when I was out and moving that I could even begin to think about Sarah again; but my attempt to think about Sarah on top of the wound-up feeling, that needing to move, was very likely the reason I had stepped out onto the street in order to avoid waiting the long turn for the traffic lights at the corner ahead – stepping out so that I could slip between the lane of stationary cars and manage those that were turning into the street where I was, but at the corner, and a little way ahead – stepping out without thinking of the empty lane between the cars in the stationary lane and myself – when I was nearly hit by a van that was moving fast between the cars and the path but which came to a stop just before I did. As if immune to what had very nearly happened – the end of my being, I was thinking now as I got to the bottom of the stairs at the station, since I had waited for that van to pass and then jaywalked from behind it – aware all the time that I continued to walk across the street despite having nearly been hit by that van, perhaps even killed, that the people in the van which had almost hit me were very likely noticing that I was continuing to cross the street as if my nearly having died was of no importance to me, even though the fact that I hadn't been hit had been a miracle of last-minute reactions, both theirs and mine, that the people in the van wouldn't have been able to help being alarmed, if they'd seen me, that I seemed to be so little affected by the narrowness of my escape, just as I, too, thinking about these possible thoughts of theirs as I walked along yesterday, was alarmed by how little I'd been affected by what could have happened, as was evident by the way my body kept going with its stepping and striding, my thoughts following afterwards as it was continuing to do right now. There was too much in my head then, I told myself as I walked up the stairs from Central station by the red-tiled wall, thinking of this bizarre reaction of mine and of how puzzled the people in the van must have been – there is always too much in my head, I had even thought yesterday, as I continued to jaywalk through the cars and vans that had almost killed me. It is a wonder, I was thinking as I mounted the stairs from the tunnel in Central station to the street, only now realising that the sharp pain I'd started to feel at the back of my heels would have to be blisters that had broken – that I have never been hit by a vehicle before – it is a wonder, in fact, that my body keeps going when most of the thoughts that I have ignore that it's there.

I had been making myself think about the manuscript yesterday after reading it and writing all one day and the next. I had wanted to try to remember the details of the manuscript that had brought me to this extraordinary breakthrough, as I would have liked to be able to tell my friend Raf last night but hadn't the courage and so knew that I never would. The manuscript had unsettled me. I'd had to move or do something straightaway, after all the reading and writing – the kind of writing that, in the past, I would never have had the nerve or sufficient limitations on my thoughts to attempt. Yesterday, I was under-slept and impatient to talk to my friend even though I was still caught up, busy with my writing – so happy to be writing at last the kind of writing that moves over water without visible sails – I was writing and all the time I was also watching myself writing; everything seemed to be possible after reading the manuscript; this was the way to write, I could see· just cutting to the quick. Sarah's manuscript was nothing at all – nothing, yes nothing at all, I could have told Raf – but the quick of it was visible everywhere on its pages. There was nothing but quick in the manuscript: quick and quick and quick. This was how I began to write yesterday. And I don't remember what I wrote, but I do remember the quick.

As I emerged onto the level of the street above the station and bent over to shove some rolled-up pieces of tissue into the backs of my shoes, it struck me that I have never let on to Raf this one desire I have always had to write a book – this one desire to bring to fruition all the years I have wasted attempting, and failing, to write the one book I have wanted to write. In fact, during all the years I have known Raf, we have spent much of our time making fun of and criticising those who have wanted to do just that, I was thinking as I paused for a minute to allow the tissue to mould to my heels, as well as to wonder which way I needed to turn to get to the café that Pamela had described: the one only half a block from Sarah's place and not far from the station, as Pamela had said

over the phone. At university, Raf and I had known so many would-be poets, would-be writers, would-be rock stars, would-be actors, and we had spent a lot of delightful hours sending up what we took to be the pathos of their plight – but that Sarah had, unbeknownst to me, fitted this type, I had never suspected, I was thinking now as I waited near the top of the stairs, still undecided about which way to cross at the lights near the station and starting, very oddly, to smile – Sarah having always struck me as the kind of person with huge potential: whose brain moves fast in bursts between the heavings of the slow, whose ruts of living become ever more deeply incised the longer they live, moving as such a person does between only one or two places and yet continuing to be capable of soaring high. I had heard of her long-term work at the Inquiries counter at a local council – the work which her mother had been pleased for her to find if nobody else – moving between these same one or two places with the great concentration that might have been brought, in other circumstances, to the unearthing of ancient treasure with brushes and finger-sized trowels, or so I was thinking as I stood at the top of the stairs – realising only then how hard Sarah would have found mounting these stairs from the station or the tunnel, these stairs being so steep and she having been so large, as Pamela had described it; Sarah would have used the escalators instead. Even then, many years ago, when we were still at school, Sarah used to move, I remember, as only someone who has become mired in a viscous dream can move – the effort immense – moving with a detached deliberation, the heaving of a determined mind – a mind which had begun to disturb me more and more the longer I knew it and which must have contributed to what had become an unquestioned, urgent need to distance my self from her in the years that followed, as if by distancing my self from her I could distance my self from what, I must have realised, was my own miring, my own deliberate movements through a dream so viscous that the movements I had already made with what had seemed immense, even super-human, efforts were nothing at all. And yet, in all these years, I had assumed Sarah was someone with a peculiar lack of interest in any kind of ambition. I myself have been obsessed since the first moments of my consciousness with the idea of making things that were significant and substantial – things which were greater than the sum bits of my self – but all the years I had known Sarah I had assumed her to be free of such an obsession; from my very earliest thoughts I have been consumed by a desire to build something out of my self, which is not my self but something else – thoughts which at the same time weigh me to the earth even as they pull me upwards and outwards – and I used to envy what I had seen as Sarah's essential freedom from these weighing, pulling thoughts. I had known Sarah to have a vast intelligence, one that dwarfed my own, but I had been astounded by how small or even non-existent were her ambitions in life – how little she thought of making anything of substance – and the idea that a person could be free of this terrible weight, this terrible and very likely self-delusional dragging and pulling, had always been a peculiar comfort and at times I had yearned to share this state. The longer that I knew her, though, this same freedom which I envied I soon began to dread – the freedom which seemed to mire her in the repetition of her days just as, in my own life, and despite my ambition, I was becoming mired without it. She had had all the world in which to move, I remember thinking back then – almost envying her in those early adult days as I shifted from one half-hearted employment to another – never committing myself to anything but only to the work, the significant work, I was going to do and yet still was not doing – that I was always going to fit around the employment that I was forced to take, as I used to think; Sarah could do anything, or so I used to believe, whereas I had always to watch my time; being free from any similar ambition, she could do anything she wanted from first waking until night, but I had always to shuffle within the compromises that I'd had to make if I were to build something out of my self that was not just my self, as I used to think it, devoting all of my time to protecting this self that I had to build. After school finished, Sarah should have been striding forth into the world and not caring about anything since she was answerable to no dream, I used to think, but instead I began to see that she was reluctant to move more than two or three steps from where she had always been. Her intelligence alone should have loosened the way for her, but instead of striding, I had seen that her steps were becoming smaller and smaller with only the deliberate meticulousness of all her actions and her sentences increasing with time. Very soon after we had left school she had found the job at the council, as I had heard from my parents, her days becoming defined by the movement between her home and the council; she could have gone to university and studied whatever she wanted, I had always thought with a detached kind of envy; she could have landed the kind of job, as they say, that saw her flitting around the world – landing in one place, as I used to think, only to be able to take off all the more lightly, without effort, with the blank and blissful mind of an enormous-faced bird. She could have been weightless with her intelligence and her freedom from ambition but instead she had somehow, definitely, become weighed to the earth, and even as I still envied her apparent somnolence I also began to suspect that despite everything, despite all of my planning and my never sleeping ambition – the ambition I had been so careful to tend at the end of my schooling and from which point of view everything had seemed so clear – I was no closer to achieving the end of this same ambition than my friend Sarah who had never, to my knowledge, desired it; and in spite of being careful always to tailor my employment around the ambition I still clung to, it was that employment itself, the journeys there and back and all the annoying minutiae between and outside these journeys, which actually used up all my time and, in fact, as I had soon begun to realise, most of my thoughts. Sarah had sunk into her work at the council and this in itself had disturbed me whenever I heard my mother mentioning it, for no other reason than for what it seemed to do to her: instead of moving to the pace of her slow but determined mind, if not high through the branches then low among the shadows, slipping always behind and between or in front,

Sarah had, early on, taken root at the council and slowly she had thickened, as if sated or diseased. No matter that I had pushed her away from me after my *religious conversion* – that I had spent years concentrating on my self – Sarah became a reminder of my failure, I was realising as I continued to stand on the footpath under the awning near the top of the stairs – not so much the failure of my resolve but of its inevitable weakness and stupidity, which had made it as unable to stand up to the world and the glamour, the distraction of radio – the one place of work that I'd thought would enable me to achieve its end – as if I had never had this ambition in the first place. Weakness and stupidity, I can see, were so much at the centre of my ambition that, in fact, they were one and the same. I had assumed all this time that Sarah, at least, had been free of this disease – a disease that constantly ate at the root of every-thing I did, everything I planned, indeed my whole view of life – a disease that I have cherished and protected, as also I have cherished and protected the anaemia I've had since childhood, I was thinking, hanging around still at the top of the stairs. All these years I have protected my ambition without questioning how I was doing it, in the same way I have protected my listlessness and pallor. For years, since I was young, I have been leached by this ambition in the same way I have been leached by my anaemia. But it has obviously suited me to be leached. There has been a glow to this leaching, a glow which I treasure; I have been as wan in the way that I have lived in the world in the same way I have been wan in my experi-ence of living, and yet this wanness, this devious leaching of my self, I have experienced as an anointing by something outside my self. I have no more been able to live without my ambition than I can live without the leaching of my blood cells – the leaching of blood cells which makes each day more difficult to live through than the day before but which gives my reflection in the mirrors and windows in the street an ever increasing mystique: a mystique which has been far more precious to me than anything else about myself that I had known until this weekend that has just passed. I have lived with my ambition in the same way I have lived with my disease: I have been in love with the perseverance of my ambition, despite the years of seeing it struggle in vain – I have been in love with it in the same way I have been in love with my increasing tiredness and the now definitely ugly parchment of my pallor. It's as if I have been watching my self in a film, I can now see – a film in which I've had to struggle but one day, soon, will shine – where the very paleness of my pallor has been the promise of that shine, of that final, glorious ending – all this time I have been in a film that I've been making in my head and at the same time I have been watching this film – I have been in love with this film I've been making and watching; I've been dreading the end even as I have been wishing every day for the shine that is to finish it. I have always hated films of this sort and yet this has been the very sort of film that I have been making in my head all these years, I have to realise now. I've always been the first to be cynical about films that end in shine, in an apotheosis of glow, but I can see that I have sacrificed years of health, years of relative happiness, just to persevere with both making and watching a film that I would have hated from the start had somebody else been making it – anybody else at all. All this should have been clear from the very beginning of my life as a thinking being, I realised, still standing on the footpath near the top of the stairs, entranced now by an old man, possibly drunk, who had pushed an empty shopping trolley to the top of the stairs from the street and was standing there with it a short way along from me, while everyone else was walking past him in a hurry to get down the stairs or up – this old man who was looking, as far as I could tell, down the stairs into the tunnel, as if to calculate how he was going to get his trolley down them one step at a time, but perhaps only thinking of something else, or just too drunk to be thinking of anything whatsoever. All this should have been clear for me to see, but until now I haven't seen it – it was not until I had read the manuscript that I could see it – and yet there was nothing in the manuscript itself about disease or ambition or films. This is the problem with my understanding of the manuscript, no matter that it fuelled my time of writing – the breakthrough, as I've been calling it, this positive breakthrough. There was no way I could begin yesterday to explain to Raf about how the manuscript had affected me, I realised, already forgetting what I had resolved to say – what had seemed easier to imagine saying when I'd been walking earlier. Either I was going to be ashamed of the failure of my memory of it, or ashamed of the feelings and realisations that had arisen from something which, on description, could only have been thought trivial and vague, no matter that I had just resolved to overcome this obstacle between us, to show my friend Raf the truth as it were. I have to think of the manuscript in a new way, I have to divorce myself from its effects, to see it as it would have appeared to anybody else who was not weighed down by the same kind of disease and ambition that the manuscript has managed to bring to the surface of me – I have to imagine, for instance, what Raf would have thought of the manuscript – or if not what he would have thought about it, how he would have described it to me. Raf has always had the most accurate and disinterested way of dissecting a book or a film. He would have described it in an interesting way: it was very likely, I was thinking, that only the bones of it would have been visible to a reader like Raf. The fact that Sarah was as diseased with the ambition to write as I have been – as the manuscript now proves by its very existence – only makes it all the more likely that a substantial amount of the manuscript would be invisible to anybody who is not so afflicted. What would be left of the narrative would be a simple description, even a tedious sequence of uninteresting events: with everything suggested, nothing pinned down. Raf would have panned the manuscript had he read it, I was realising as I stood, still watching the man – the drunk – with the trolley that was already teetering at the top of the stairs – someone should go to the man and get that trolley, I was thinking but still failing to move to do anything about it; if that trolley gets loose, someone will get hurt or even killed – at best Raf would have argued against its premises; at worst sent it up – or more – it was very likely he would never have succumbed to reading it, or even accepting it to read, in the first instance. I can imagine him saying that he would have left the manuscript at the wake – that he would not have been at all fazed by appearing to seem so heartless at such a time, because only in that way would he not have been lying to everyone around him as well as to himself.

And yet the manuscript is a great achievement, I was thinking again, now that I'd got out my phone again to check the directions in Pamela's text and turned from the old man (no longer caring about what happened to the trolley or anyone in its path), and was walking again so I could catch the green pedestrian lights to cross the street – remembering the quick of it and the quick of its effects on Saturday and Sunday, on that writing I had done, the breakthrough as I'd been calling it – the manuscript as an extraordinary achievement, and all the more since it has arisen from someone who appeared to have no longing, no wish for such an achievement at all. It is, in fact, the kind of achievement that my friend Raf would approve of, I told myself as I got to the pedestrian island, since it is the kind of achievement that seems to have come from nowhere and yet to arrive in the world all at once, and without antecedents. All the years when we have made fun of the would-be artists and would-be poets, we have never made fun of achievements such as this: where the artist or writer, never dreaming of success, produces something unique, which, nevertheless, is little praised by anybody except ourselves and the odd foreign name. If the artwork or writing is unfashionable, it is very likely that the artwork or writing will be praised by us and hailed as a gem; if it is fashionable or, worse, betrays a yearning to be fashionable, we are fast with condemnation, firm with our blows. When an artist slaves for art and then dies before the art can be admired properly by the masses, as our understanding tells us – that is the kind of artwork we respect beyond a doubt – but even within the oeuvre of an artist it is never the later loved artworks that we love, only the unloved ones; not Kafka's *Metamorphosis*, for example, but his 'The Burrow' or 'A Hunger Artist'; never Van Gogh's later, luminous coloured fields but the turgid, weighted lines of his earliest drawings. Sarah's manuscript has, in fact, all the hallmarks of an artwork we would love. If my good friend Raf could only get to see it in this way, I was thinking, he would love the manuscript: he would become its connoisseur.

While I walked along the side of the Dental Hospital, whose dim, double-hung windows made it impossible not to think of the pain that was being inflicted, as I was imagining, just metres from my face, I tried to think of my old friend Sarah as I had seen her in Rockdale and once or twice much earlier on – as a large – yes, increasingly heavy, ponderous person, with her curt, passionate ideas pressing through lips so immobile they might have been numb like mine get to be – Sarah that, all the time, had seemed so preoccupied with her job at the council that she would talk of nothing else. And yet all the time, too, I have to realise, she must have been wanting to write something of significance in the way I have always wanted to do such a thing for myself; she had grown large and vegetal at the council and in her movements and all the time, without my knowing it, she had simultaneously been working on something so unusual, so moving, that its rhythm has crept into my thoughts and everything that I do; I left my flat with it still in my veins after that reading and writing, I was thinking now, remembering my walk to the shops on the Sunday afternoon – my walk that was filled to the brim with the conviction that at last I had discovered something important – this conviction running all through my body, enlivening my blood. It was her greatest coup, if she could have known it – it was certainly her greatest coup that she should have fooled me all those years into thinking that she had been wasting her time and her life at the council when really she had been spending those same years, as it seems now, working on something that I might have wanted to work on myself, perfecting what I could only have wanted to perfect by myself. When I continued to cross the four lanes of traffic after the near accident yesterday afternoon – after taking my life into my hands, as it's put, for no obvious reason – I began to be curious about how untouched I am by all that's around me. I had been so taken in by the manuscript, not so much unable to put it down but unable to leave it alone, that at the end of the reading, and all of the writing that proceeded from the reading, I had – and continue to have – no sense at all of what the manuscript is about. It has moved me, I had been thinking as I continued on my walk to the supermarket to shop for the dinner with Raf, and was thinking again now as I crossed Elizabeth Street and then turned at the bank into Foveaux Street on my way to meet Pamela – I have been moved by something in the manuscript that has got me to write. I have taken in every word, I know, but, in fact, I am aware that I cannot recall a single phrase or sentence, anything concrete. All the time that I was striding up the escalator to the supermarket yesterday, overtaking everyone who was standing in my way, I was thinking of the manuscript and its extraordinary effect, and yet at the same time I knew that I was going to make fun of this manuscript that I had at last got around to reading: I had told my friend Raf on the phone that something strange had happened that week – the word 'strange' being code, as we both knew, for an interesting bit of news that I could relay to him as soon as we saw each other – the teaser on the phone somehow diffusing the tale even as it enhanced the anticipation of it – the word 'strange' getting turned over and over in my brain as I passed through the automatic opening gates at the supermarket, and making it easier to keep the whole of what I was going to say forwards in my mind even as the word itself kept me from thinking of the very real strangeness of the manuscript as clearly as I might have done. I had thought 'strange' and thought of myself thinking this word, excited by the word and everything that it suggested; my mind funnelling down through the air above me onto this word, as it seems to be doing to me now in Surry Hills, funnelling down onto this word 'strange' from some distance above, as from that darkening white of the sky above the house party: onto 'strange' and everything that it suggested and everything that I had intended to say and so what I have only ever wanted to say to Raf: *strange, strange, strange, strange.* And yet I knew then that, if I did so, the entire time that I tried to describe the manuscript in this light, there would be something false in my voice that would be impossible to miss: in the supermarket I had thought of the story I would tell – about the ridiculousness of what had happened – of how despite everything I had gone and read the manuscript after all – of how I had been unable to resist reading the manuscript once I had been expressly asked not to read it – of how perverse I was (enjoying thinking of this word 'perverse' once more). But I had known then that I would falter the moment I was asked to describe the quality of the manuscript (since I knew I couldn't describe its effects as it was impossible to describe them unless to send them up – to send them up or to reveal that I was writing again – or that I was even writing at all) – how just to pronounce the word 'manuscript' in a serious tone, whether to Pamela or to Raf, would be to undo something important: the magic of it all gone – my words, my writing, come to an end.

I had stopped walking the moment I had this thought in the supermarket, I was remembering now as I limped along – my right heel smarting more than my left – limping past a series of windows, on the other side of the street, that had huge, apparently joyous images of singers taking up all of the glass along the footpath; I hadn't taken another step forwards among the shoppers in the supermarket but had stood for a moment and made as if to fumble first at my sleeve for my watch, and then in my bag, my mind looking on, as it always does, in moments like these. I am being ridiculous, I remember thinking as I went to the refrigerated section, hoping to jog my mind so that it might move forwards again. Don't be silly, I had to tell myself, almost out loud: I don't want to keep the manuscript, it means nothing to me – it's completely nothing and not a talisman at all. I took a bag of mixed leaves and put it in the basket I'd collected at the gates; I got prosciutto from the deli and stood for a minute at the seafood section, wondering about prawns and the shelling and the muck in their backs that takes ages to get out. The sooner I give the manuscript back to Pamela on Monday the sooner I can relax, I thought as I looked at the prawns; the sooner I pass on the manuscript, keeping cool in my deception, the sooner I might continue to write as I seem to have been writing – the breakthrough becoming a breakthrough indeed, I was thinking and hoping.

I finished reading the manuscript at half past two in the morning on Saturday, I was remembering as I pushed myself to walk up the sloping street despite my enormous tiredness now and the blisters that had definitely burst on my heels; to keep walking, when every step slices into my flesh, even to the bone, I was thinking – to continue on my way up what has to be a forty-five degree incline, soon to arrive at the corner of the street that is supposed to have the café on it, where I can plonk the manuscript in front of the sister and go away again, perhaps on to work (in a taxi next). I finished it the first time on Saturday, and then after a short pause of trying to sleep, I started it again – I was in a daze, I thought now, thinking of that night – I was crazy to have started again on the manuscript; if I had known how much I would be affected just by reading it (so restless now since the breakthrough, unable to sleep) I might have preferred to leave it alone – no matter that I would have forgone the breakthrough and everything that has followed from it. If I had left the manuscript where it was that first evening, I would very likely have had three nights of uneventful sleep and restful days, I was thinking as I got closer, higher up the sloping street, to the corner where the café was supposed to be. I would have come in to Surry Hills as promised, no doubt – but only just in time and by bus or car – to have a chat with the sister as she wanted (allowing her to pay, just to wreak my vengeance for everything she'd done to me in the past) and then gone on to work at the radio station, still warm with the after-effects of the admiration that I would have tapped from her perfumed chest from mentioning (wickedly, intentionally) a name like Cate and some reference to a film. I might have got annoyed at having to see the sister again – because of those thoughts about the house party and the way I had succumbed to the lures of her second-hand, over-emotive words – but I would have profited, too, concocting anecdotes for Raf; I would still have kept on and on, trying to get down to my old kind of writing and continuing to fail – but so I had all my life – what was new? – all of us read this kind of writing that I was trying to write before I had read this manuscript, whatever we think we do; we hate it, but it's what we read; there is little else, even if we cannot bear – we always stop ourselves – to write it down. My life would have been calm and quotidian, even beautiful, I was thinking – none of these megalomaniac thoughts, nothing disturbed.

Because, yes: as I moved through the flat when I had finished re-reading the manuscript on Saturday morning, I found myself moving as if I were living the manuscript in everything that I did. Even the radio news, when it came on with the alarm that I had forgotten to turn off, was filtered through the rhythms of the manuscript, which was all, in the end, I kept hold of just then, and so the extraordinary news about the Premier and his belief in the panthers – the panthers that are said to wander the Blue Mountains – the odd coincidence of this news that stayed long in my mind and through everything that I wrote that day – the news padding a long, determined path in my brain as only a panther might be able to do. Even the government has started to believe in the panthers, I remember thinking – not as surprised by the coincidence of the news as I should have been, the coincidence of the panthers – the extraordinary coincidence of the panthers and the manuscript, but even then, despite my determination to write against it, I thought of the panthers and the Blue Mountains – the vast uninhabited tracts of the Blue Mountains. I have always wanted to live in the mountains, I remember thinking after Raf had gone home last night: it has always been in the mountains, in the drenched, sweet dark of a gully *somewhere else* that I have imagined being able to write, and so it was in this way that, clicking closed the document I'd opened the day before, I started to trawl the pictures of houses for sale in the Blue Mountains on the internet. All these years I have made nothing but compromises with my life, I had been telling myself as I searched, surprised, too, perhaps, that I was not concerned I was wasting my precious time for writing. In the wake of the manuscript, of my breakthrough – or should I say despite the manuscript and my breakthrough, I was thinking now – I was determined to risk everything: my work, my friendship with Raf, the small stability of my life in my rented flat in Glebe, so that for once, I had thought as I filled in an online application for finance from my bank – for once I might be putting my writing self first, as I have always wanted to do; this time I might commit myself, to buying my chance to live in a writerly house in a writerly location, so that more and more I'd be able to write in the way I had just been doing. No compromises anymore, I had told myself as I typed my current address into the boxes on the screen. If the commuting becomes too much I can always leave work. If Raf makes fun of me – whether to my face or to his vast group of friends I have never met – it will be too late: I will already have the house and be writing far away from him. In the end there will be this writerly house in the mountains, and the writing – nothing is going to divert me from my path towards the fulfilment of my writing, I had been thinking as I searched through the Domain section of the online *Herald* and other real estate sites last night. All this reminds me now, I was thinking as I got nearer to the Crown Street corner – reminds me of that time, nearly eight or ten years ago when, in a fury after an argument with someone at the studio, I had driven westwards from work, not even stopping at home for clothes or a toothbrush, the whole way thinking of the Carrington at Katoomba where, for a night, I imagined myself indulging in the belief that I was living a hundred years ago or more – before my colleague was born – and that my life could therefore begin again as I am always hoping it will. Nothing is going to divert me from what I know I have to do for my self, I'd been thinking as I drove – feeling totally pissed off at the comments he'd made and the comments I'd made – remembering everything that I'd said or been thinking for months and, of course, about my non-existent writing, all the frustrations with my writing, which, back then, I was blaming him and his nit-picking perfectionism for. But, of course, the sign 'Panthers and the Museum of Fire Use Route Number Fourteen' had emerged from the side of the road once the mountains were in view. I was out on a road towards a night that I hadn't expected that morning – being, for once, *totally spontaneous*, as I had been thinking – driving away from a bungle, an embarrassment – and drunk, as it seemed, with the idea that I could drive in this way, by taking nothing and everything, following my nose – and so all signs were signs for me, they all spoke to me as signs, I was remembering as I got at last to the top of Foveaux Street – the top of the hill and also, as it happened, to the set of lights that was nearly opposite the café where I was heading. I had been driving towards the mountains – towards a sign of authenticity, which was the mountains for me, somehow, and the Carrington (I'd been there for a wedding the previous October, I remember, and been impressed by the leadlight windows and, of course, by the views) – but the beauty of the traffic sign had entranced me and in my drunken state, I had been lured from the road. Perhaps I had been expecting a miracle, I was thinking now as I looked at the café and what might have been Pamela inside it, my heart still pounding from the walk up the hill. I am always seeing signs but never following them, I had told myself. I remember diverging from the motorway, curious about this 'fourteen' and what 'Panthers' *really was* and thinking: I never do anything for my self. All these years I have put up with an imperfect life. All these years I have put up with scummy flats and high and ever increasing rents, irritating workmates, the tainted damp of a sterile city – and all for what, I had been asking myself over and over as I drove along the fourteen, on this apparently small diversion from my way. Until this moment of spontaneity I thought I knew the ways of my mind, I had told myself as I drove: I knew I woke up early in the mornings once the days, dilating in the spring, pressed inwards, into the night – I knew I would lie awake during the nights, too, trying to catch myself meandering from the logic in my thoughts, waiting for the visits of the impossible, the strange, the unlikely, the irrational, because it was only then that I could sink into the sweet, sweet nothing of sleep. All these years I have known how certain women behind clothes shop counters affect me – how, when they wait with the trousers I have chosen in their hands, looking down at a screen as they listen for the scanned bar code to register, they are likely to be wondering why it is that I had criticised the cut of the trousers even as I was handing over my credit card to them because, unbeknownst to them – or so I have always assumed – and to say more would only make the matter far, far worse, I would be thinking – the way they keep to the other side of the counter and watch me, looking up from the screen, has always made me think that they are surprised or critical of my choice or my size, my hair or the mole on my forehead – I have known that I would never change lanes on the highway unless doing so could mean that I wouldn't have to change lanes a few kilometres ahead – I have known that some people arouse in me a distaste that I can never explain and much less justify – I have known that in the end – in those days I had often been thinking about the end, for some reason, I was realising, even though the procedure recommended by the doctor to investigate the cause of my anaemia was only a *minor procedure*, as if all I had to do was fill out a couple of forms – it has seemed as if my whole life until that moment of the sign has been a gradual adjustment in my thinking about the end and this its only purpose – that in the end I will slowly lose all grip on the necessities of washing, cooking, cleaning and organising, and that instead I will sit in a chair by a window, watching a branch with soft variegated leaves knock against a handrail. I remember that I had already decided that the peak of my life had passed me by while I was standing on a bus going somewhere, sleeping on the sofa or reading an article in the newspaper while standing up in the kitchen – those times when I skipped most of the article because I couldn't be bothered – and had therefore decided that now, since the end was coming as it would, there was no point trying to make any efforts to change how I was anymore. This is how I have always been, I remember thinking as I drove towards Panthers – and this many years before reading Sarah's manuscript, I was thinking now as I crossed the road towards the café and the sister – I look to the left and to the right looking out for panthers – yes, I have always been on the look-out for panthers, I told myself as I thought of my self leaning forwards at the computer last night, too exhausted to think of houses anymore, too tired to sleep – my head on my arm, thinking again of the title: *Panthers and the Museum of Fire* – the sign at which I had veered from the road – always seeking the panthers: one panther and another but, of course, finding nothing, or even less than nothing – a computer full of real estate copy, a wasted night.

I had driven out to Panthers instead of the Blue Mountains. It was small wonder that I wanted to see this place, this Panthers, for myself because all those years, whenever I had driven towards the mountains I had always wanted to see what Panthers might look like, but had never dared. I want to look it in the face, I remember thinking as I drove by the sign and so veered off the motorway into the dark. I drove first to Panthers and then to the Museum of Fire: first to Panthers with its great, wide car park ticking under a sun that had already set, and then, further on, to the museum, which was closed, the whole place quiet and dull and oddly very sad. It says everything about my life thus far, this hunting of panthers and museums of fire, I was thinking as I thought of my self sitting in the museum car park then, too dazed, too disappointed to get out – all this says everything about me and my life, I had thought, too, all those years ago, when I wasn't even thinking about my writing quite, and I can't help thinking now, I realised as I looked at this café that was only half a block away from where Sarah had been living, as Pamela had told me on the phone on Friday – I discovered this place *that day*, she had said, *that unfortunate day*. There have been times at work when I might have stepped forwards and allowed myself to be taken up by ordinary things, the ordinary activities of doing a good job – when I might have thrown myself into my work and the life of my one good friend with the ardour and talent that I've reserved for my supposed writing – but the thought of everything that is suggested by signs like 'Panthers and the Museum of Fire' – by which I mean my writing – has always taken precedence, and ironically it has been this obsession with the nebulous life of signs that has stopped all possibility of doing any kind of serious or interesting writing, I was thinking, as I remembered how long into the night I looked at the houses on the internet on the Sunday night, turning the computer off only when my right-hand forefinger was getting sore and tingling from scrolling the pages of houses in gullies, all the houses in the gullies that I thought I could afford. I have spent years doing nothing but trying to further my obsession with becoming a writer and it's all been a distraction, I was thinking as I walked across the street that Sarah had lived on once, apparently: all the time I have believed my self to be the protagonist of a writing story – the story of a writer – the kind of story that is as mysterious and alluring as the title of Sarah's manuscript – a protagonist who herself writes stories that are similarly mysterious and alluring. All the time, wanting to be this kind of writer rather than the one that is staring at my father in his study mirror, that rust-spotted mirror in his writing room under the stairs – where every day he gets up from the couch he keeps in the room for the purpose of *resting his eyes* and washes out his socks and his underpants in the garage sink so that his wife (my mother) will have no excuse to *intrude on his writing space* – where every day since his retirement from Pennant Hills High School he's sat in his corduroys at his desk in the room under the stairs and stared at his ancient IBM with the DOS instructions and the half-dead printer (whose ribbon he re-inks by hand, purpling his reddening, calcifying, blistering fingers – his circulation slowing down), trying to get out the writing, as he puts it, this writing that is killing him, this writing that is the cancer that is destroying his life, which fouls his breath, which drives away his only child and falsifies his wife, which has constructed a warren of impossibilities around him: the yellow of the clippings he's kept in shoe boxes and plastic bags, the photographs he's stacked in feathering, half-rotted boxes near the window that looks out onto the cleft in the gully, the volumes of books he's stolen from the library, the despairing hunger of his writing, which is the only edge that it has, that he raises each morning to cut into his festering body but never gets anywhere near the centre of what he's trying to get at no matter how many thousands and thousands of words he writes, as he says, and as I was telling myself as I limped into the café, this place that fitted the terse description – wooden windows, little stools – that Pamela had given it.

Whereas, I might have hovered near the counter for some minutes, as I usually do, trying to work out whether I should be placing my order there or taking a seat instead so that I might order from the table, I now found my self stepping towards the counter, wondering at my stepping forwards at this point, even as I was stepping, and the apparent ease with which I spoke the few but necessary words – *a double-shot latte to have here* – and then going to sit somewhere near the window – a table for two: Pamela, the sister, to be by the window, my self looking out; all the decisions, suddenly, running ahead of me, as it was seeming – my body and my voice all on their own. I caught my self removing a damp, folded newspaper – removing it so that I could put the manuscript in its Aldi bag in front of me – my hands working ahead, my thoughts catching up – removing the newspaper, presumably, so that the manuscript might be seen to be sitting there in front of me when Pamela came – the newspaper already moved to another table, the manuscript in front of me: too late to change them back. Look what my hands do even without my prompting them, I could have said to anyone who would listen. I looked down again at the manuscript, the manuscript that was seen to be lying in front of me – lying there in front of me, I realised, so that Pamela can be assured when she arrives, without having to ask, that I had not forgotten to bring the very thing that she had asked for, even though I had gone against her wishes by reading it, and also by spending hours and hours after closing the computer last night photographing each page of the manuscript too, so I might not lose this thing, this nothing, without which I am nothing at all. I am a coward, I told my self in the café then, a pure coward. But even as I was thinking this, too, I noticed that I had failed to remove the manuscript and hide it in my shoulder bag, as I should have done. When it comes to it, my first reaction is always to appease, I was thinking – I will be drowned in a flood of appeasement one day (I saw that my hands were resting on either side of the manuscript, the palms faced upwards and the fingers relaxed) – one day there will be nothing left of me but gestures like this – gestures which mime a perfect, open, relaxed state of being, but, in fact, I can see, lie over a wide, grey sea, an ocean, of agitation – gestures which continue the folding of ourselves into the abject and hypocritical stances of appeasement that women like me seem automatically to do, without any encouragement; gestures which should immediately be driven from our repertoire of actions in the world; which should always be suspected, and particularly between women; gestures which are the equivalent of the hand concealing the pistol in the coat; gestures which should be frisked for in public spaces such as this one; which should be questioned the moment that they appear – is there a valid reason for this gesture, madam? On a rating of one to ten, how well do you wish the world? I am afraid I have found you guilty of wilfully manufacturing a deceiving gesture. Between your gesture and the truth is a vast and frightening, sentimental space.

I had pictured myself sitting in the café looking out onto the street – looking out onto the street as a writer would and no longer as only a would-be writer would. I have ordered a coffee, as I expected to do, and then sat down near the windows – these windows a lot brighter than the windows I'd imagined – much brighter and far more cheerful, since there's a long sheet of light lying out there on the asphalt, on top of the road – but I hadn't thought further than this. This is the café that's closest to Sarah's place, as Pamela had said – Sarah would have passed by this café every day, very likely; in the evenings as she sat at her desk, or on her bed, after work at the council, she must even have had thoughts about this café as she wrote; everything that you experience becomes part of your writing, I was thinking, even if everything that you write is a complete fabrication. Of course, it was Sarah who wrote the manuscript, I then thought as I looked down at the Aldi bag that was still lying on the table in front of me. I can hardly remember this person, this Sarah. When I imagined my self waiting for Pamela at the café I'd pictured my self sitting at a window, as I was doing now, a notebook in front of me; with the manuscript and a notebook, even though, in fact, I never usually use notebooks or even pens and paper, only screens; both of them in front of me: the manuscript and the notebook that I failed to buy at the newsagency – which I stopped myself buying at the newsagency. But I haven't been able to think about Sarah. Every time I try to think about Sarah I remember nothing more than some edges of vaguest thoughts, as well as everything that I have ever said to anybody else about her: all of my lies and exaggerations. The more I try to think about her, the more these lies and exaggerations come to the fore. But she was the one who wrote this manuscript, I now thought as a waiter placed a double-shot latte on the table to the right of the manuscript. She was the one that wrote this manuscript, *Panthers and the Museum of Fire* – the title a trap, a deliberate trap, a lure – or just a provocation – sitting in her room in Surry Hills overlooking this café, as I now tried to picture it even though I could see no houses from here; quite a lot larger, as her sister had described her; and then I flicked open this manuscript to which I owe my breakthrough – the manuscript which, as it turned out, I only had a few minutes to look at again before Pamela arrived in a coat that reminded me of something that Sarah might have worn in those days when we used to hang out in her garden – this manuscript whose contents will always escape me, and all the more so as I write now, four years later, when even the sign on the motorway has long been replaced – the 'Panthers' erased and also the number of the route – and the photographs of the manuscript that were lost in a single instant when I scraped the SD card as I pulled it out of the camera to have my images of the manuscript printed at Officeworks – writing, I see now, that is no longer anything approaching a continuation of the immediate euphoria of reading but only the attempt to remember the effect of the manuscript on me – my writing only a remembering of a remembering of that reading and writing, no matter that I continue to think of it as a breakthrough – this manuscript whose existence, as soon as I learned of it, I feared and loathed and never had any intention of reading in the first place.